Kelsey Armstrong Waters stared at her reflection in the three-way mirror and grinned. The vintage lace veil looked as if it had been woven specifically for the porcelain flower wreath she'd found in Paris. Any one of Kelsey's brides would consider herself fortunate to wear the exquisite pieces.

She adjusted the veil slightly. Oh, my. Kelsey blinked. Once. Twice.

The unbelievable happened. She looked like a bride. An unexpected rush of emotion overtook her. But not even catching her cousin's wedding bouquet or wearing this breathtaking headpiece would change what she already knew in her heart to be true. Marriage wasn't for her. Not now, not ever.

The sound of a male voice sent a shiver down her spine. Standing in the doorway was a man dressed in khakis, a white shirt and a brown leather jacket.

This is the man I'm going to marry.

Dear Reader,

I'm dreaming of summer vacations—of sitting by the beach, dangling my feet in a lake, walking on a mountain or curling up in a hammock. And in each vision, I have a Silhouette Romance novel, and I'm happy. Why don't you grab a couple and join me? And in each book take a look at our Silhouette Makes You a Star contest!

We've got some terrific titles in store for you this month. Longtime favorite author Cathie Linz has developed some delightful stories with U.S. Marine heroes and *Stranded with the Sergeant* is appealing and fun. Cara Colter has the second of her THE WEDDING LEGACY titles for you. *The Heiress Takes a Husband* features a rich young woman who's struggling to prove herself—and the handsome attorney who lends a hand.

Arlene James has written over fifty titles for Silhouette Books, and her expertise shows. *So Dear to My Heart* is a tender, original story of a woman finding happiness again. And Karen Rose Smith—another popular veteran—brings us *Doctor in Demand*, about a wounded man who's healed by the love of a woman and her child.

And two newer authors round out the list! Melissa McClone's *His Band of Gold* is an emotional realization of the power of love, and Sue Swift debuts in Silhouette Romance with *His Baby, Her Heart,* in which a woman agrees to fulfill her late sister's dream of children. It's an unusual and powerful story that is part of our THE BABY'S SECRET series.

Enjoy these stories, and make time to appreciate yourselves in your hectic lives! Have a wonderful summer.

Happy reading!

Mary-Theresa Hussey

Mary-Theresa Hussey
Senior Editor

Please address questions and book requests to:
Silhouette Reader Service
U.S.: 3010 Walden Ave., P.O. Box 1325, Buffalo, NY 14269
Canadian: P.O. Box 609, Fort Erie, Ont. L2A 5X3

His Band of Gold

MELISSA McCLONE

SILHOUETTE *Romance*

Published by Silhouette Books

America's Publisher of Contemporary Romance

To Louise Vernon
and her Wednesday night group:
Barbara, Jenny, Laurie, Linda and Shirley.

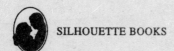 SILHOUETTE BOOKS

ISBN 0-373-19537-0

HIS BAND OF GOLD

Copyright © 2001 by Melissa Martinez McClone

This edition published by arrangement with Harlequin Books S.A.

® and TM are trademarks of Harlequin Books S.A., used under license. Trademarks indicated with ® are registered in the United States Patent and Trademark Office, the Canadian Trade Marks Office and in other countries.

Visit Silhouette at www.eHarlequin.com

Printed in U.S.A.

Books by Melissa McClone

Silhouette Romance

If the Ring Fits... #1431
The Wedding Lullaby #1485
His Band of Gold #1537

Yours Truly

Fiancé for the Night

MELISSA McCLONE

With a degree in mechanical engineering from Stanford University, the last thing Melissa McClone ever thought she would be doing is writing romance novels, but analyzing engines for a major U.S. airline just couldn't compete with her "happily-ever-afters."

When she isn't writing, caring for her two young children or doing laundry, Melissa loves to curl up on the couch with a cup of tea, her cats and a good book. She is also a big fan of *The X-Files* and enjoys watching home decorating shows to get ideas for her house—a 1939 cottage that is *slowly* being renovated.

Melissa lives in Lake Oswego, Oregon, with her own real-life hero husband, daughter, son, two lovable but oh-so-spoiled indoor cats and a no-longer-stray outdoor kitty who decided to call the garage home. Melissa loves to hear from readers. You can write to her at P.O. Box 63, Lake Oswego, OR 97034.

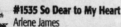

Prologue

"**Y**ou know what this means, don't you?" The beaming princess bride, Her Serene Highness Christina Armstrong de Thierry of San Montico, didn't give Kelsey time to answer. "You'll be the next one to get married."

"No." Kelsey Armstrong Waters stared at the breathtaking all-white royal bridal bouquet in her hands. The sweet scent of the roses tickled her nostrils as if the flowers got the joke. The last thing she'd intended to do was to catch the damn bouquet, but before she knew what was happening she had. Her first thought had been to let it fall to the ground, but as maid of honor—not to mention a wedding consultant herself—she couldn't allow that to happen. Nor would she allow herself to buy into that silly myth. Not even for her favorite cousin. "I won't be getting married."

"You say that now." Christina gazed longingly at her handsome husband, Prince Richard de Thierry, and her smile widened. "Just wait until you meet Mr. Right. Trust me, you'll change your mind. Fast."

Kelsey didn't want to spoil her cousin's perfect wedding day so she held her tongue. The institution of marriage might be perfect for Christina and many others, but it would never be for Kelsey. "Why don't you toss it again so someone else can catch it and not ruin any...traditions?"

"You won't be able to stop this tradition from coming true." Christina was practically floating three feet off the ground in the crowded ballroom. Given her fairy-tale romance and royal wedding, no one could blame her, including Kelsey. It was hard for even the most cynical not to get caught up in the magical atmosphere. No doubt this was one couple who would live happily ever after. Christina sighed. "There's something about the magical power of love..."

Magic was one thing, but love? Forget it. Kelsey knew firsthand that the majority of marriages failed. Her parents and many of her clients were nothing more than statistics. Marriage was as easy as saying "I do," but divorce was even easier. All it took was an "I don't." A sad but true fact of life. And one she never wanted to be a part of. Ever. "I only caught the bouquet. I didn't get the royal engagement ring stuck on my finger like you did."

"Doesn't matter."

As Christina waved her left hand in the air, the enchanted ring that had brought her and her prince together acted as a prism, sending a colorful spectrum of light flashing. The sparkles landed on wedding guests as if the ring were spreading its magic on all it touched. Kelsey took a step back to avoid being hit, but the light still managed to flash on the bouquet in her hands. Better the flowers than her.

"You won't have any choice," Christina continued. "One day your own Prince Charming will enter your life and the next thing you know you'll be married."

That only happened in fairy tales. And for Christina. Kelsey couldn't help but smile at her favorite cousin's good fortune. But *she* was another story.

Kelsey might want a boyfriend, but a husband?

Forget it.

Too much hassle.

Too much trouble.

Too much heartache.

She tightened her grip on the bouquet. "Don't forget, I'm never getting married."

"Never say never." Christina grinned. "Trust me on this one, okay?"

Chapter One

January 31

A perfect match.

Kelsey Armstrong Waters stared at her reflection in the three-way mirror and grinned. The vintage lace veil she'd purchased in London looked as if it had been woven specifically for the pearl, diamond and porcelain flower wreath she'd found in Paris. A satisfied feeling settled in the center of her chest. Any one of Kelsey's brides would consider herself fortunate to wear the exquisite pieces.

She adjusted the veil slightly. Oh, my. Kelsey blinked. Once. Twice.

The unbelievable happened. She looked like a bride and felt like one, too. Glowing, radiant, you name it. Love, happily-ever-after, even magic seemed to fill the room. An unexpected rush of emotion overtook her. Kelsey sighed.

Was this how all those brides felt when they found "the" gown to wear? Was this what caused the tears to spike their lashes and their smiles to widen? Was this it?

She took a deep breath and smelled the sweet scent of roses, but that wasn't possible. The only roses in her office were the dried blossoms from the royal wedding bouquet she'd caught, preserved and put on display for her clients to see. It was her one perk for catching the flowers—the pop culture value of having a piece of history from the royal wedding.

Thinking about the bouquet made her think of her cousin. No doubt Christina would have a good laugh if she saw Kelsey right now. On second thought, Christina would probably be thrilled and tell Kelsey what a lovely bride she'll be when she finally walked down the aisle herself.

But that wasn't about to happen. Not even catching the wedding bouquet or wearing this breathtaking headpiece would change what she already knew in her heart to be true. Marriage wasn't for her. Not now, not ever.

Frowning, she stared at her reflection once again. Trying on the veil and wreath had been a stupid idea. "Why didn't I just eat a two pound bag of peanut M&M's instead?"

"I prefer plain myself." The one-hundred-percent male voice sent a shiver down her spine.

Even though she was alone, she didn't feel threatened. Having a suite of offices in one of the most exclusive buildings in Beverly Hills afforded her some security. Kelsey turned.

Standing in the doorway of the reception area was a man dressed in a pair of khakis, a white oxford shirt and a brown leather jacket. Casual yet classic. A man's man kind of outfit. And that hair... His deep brown—almost-black—hair fell just above his jacket collar and was brushed back off his forehead as if it were a careless afterthought.

He was, in a word—spectacular. Considering her aptly earned title, "Wedding Consultant to the Stars," that was saying something. He could have been a model except for the slightly crooked nose that gave his face personality. Lots of personality. Kelsey smiled. His chiseled cheekbones could have only been sculpted by a great artist. His full lips hinted of hot, slow kisses. And his eyes made her feel as if she were the most important woman in the world.

This is the man I'm going to marry.

The thought came from out of nowhere, and she tried to understand the motivating factor behind it. She'd been surrounded by gorgeous men most of her life and knew better than to be taken in by a pretty face. Still, his relaxed stance and easy smile appealed to her on a gut level.

He'd hardly said five words, but his charm reached across the expanse of her office. Too bad she hadn't heard bells when she first saw him, then she'd know...

Know what? That she was acting like a teenager with her first crush? "May I help you?"

"I'm looking for Kelsey Waters." He smiled, a charming smile that showed off straight white teeth, and her legs turned to linguini. Okay, she was a sucker for a great smile.

"I—I..." Hoping to quell the butterflies churning up her stomach, she breathed deeply and exhaled. Slowly. She couldn't remember the last time a man—any man—had her so tongue-tied, and she didn't like it. She was

twenty-six years old, not thirteen. Time to get control.
"I'm Kelsey Armstrong Waters."

"So you're the one I've been looking for."

Her breath caught in her throat. Breathe, she ordered
herself. Just breathe. "How can I help you?"

"I need help planning a wedding."

Reality hit Kelsey, low and hard. The handsome
stranger was a potential client—someone else's groom.

Disappointment shot through her. Not that she per-
sonally wanted a groom. Maybe she could borrow him
for a date or two. What was she thinking? Oh, boy, she
needed a vacation more than she realized. Time away
from nervous brides and jittery grooms and treasury-
breaking weddings... Only a few more hours until her
flight.

She forced a smile. "And you are...?"

"Will." As he walked toward her, he grinned. The
smile crinkled the corners of his green eyes and made
him even more appealing. "Will Addison."

Addison. The name sounded familiar, but she hadn't
met him before. She knew that for certain.

"Nice to meet you." She forced the words from her
drier-than-dry mouth and extended her right arm. As his
hand touched hers, tingles shot up her arm and straight
down to the tips of her leather pumps.

Ignore the tingles, Kelsey told herself. Concentrate
on something else, anything else. Like his handshake.
His handshake was solid, firm, as was the man in front
of her. She was nearly five-nine, but she felt almost
petite standing in front of his six-foot-plus frame. Re-
alizing she'd allowed the handshake to last longer than
was appropriate, she pulled her hand away.

"Nice veil," Will said in that deep, warm voice of
his. "You'll make a lovely bride."

A bride? Kelsey touched the top of her head. Great, she still had the headpiece on. She could only imagine how ridiculous she looked in the getup. The least he could have done was mention it earlier so she didn't look like such a fool. Kelsey removed the wreath and veil and set them on a nearby table. "I'm not getting married. Just trying them on. I like to keep certain one-of-a-kind items in stock for my clients."

"Whatever bride wears that veil will be one lucky lady."

The compliment warmed her cheeks. What was happening to her? She wasn't the blushing type.

"What can I do for you?" The words came out sounding husky, a way she hadn't meant them to sound.

"My sister's getting married and wants you to co-ordinate her wedding."

His sister. Kelsey's pulse picked up speed, racing faster than a car chase on the 101. The knowledge that Will Addison wasn't the groom-to-be made her feel as though one of her weddings had been featured on "Weddings of a Lifetime." She really did need a vacation if this was what a handsome stranger could do to her. Kelsey motioned him to the area where she consulted with clients. "Why don't you have a seat?"

"Thanks." Will sat in one of the overstuffed chintz-covered down chairs. "Nice place."

"Thanks." He should have looked out of place among all the feminine decor and bridal accessories, but he didn't. Not one bit. And it annoyed Kelsey. This was her turf, her home field advantage, so to speak. Yet he didn't seem uncomfortable among all the ruffles, ribbons and frills. "So when…"

As he picked up one of the bride magazines from the table and set it back down, Kelsey caught a flash of gold. She glanced at his left hand. At the ring finger of his left hand. At the gold wedding band on his ring finger.

Married. The man of her dreams was somebody else's husband. No doubt another woman had realized he was a keeper. Yet he had flirted—well, maybe not flirted, but he'd—

Stop it.

This wasn't like her. Not one bit. Will Addison was not the man of her dreams. Such a man didn't exist. Kelsey of all people knew better than to engage in any sort of romantic fantasy. Not even for the briefest of moments. And definitely not with a married man. She straightened. "When is your sister's big day, Mr. Addison?"

"Friends call me Will."

"I'm sure they do." Business demeanor back in place, Kelsey pulled out the five-year calendar planner from a nearby shelf and flipped it open. "So when does your sister want to get married?"

"February fourteenth."

"I'm already booked for next year."

"Not next year." As he leaned toward her, she caught a whiff of him. Soap and water and something woodsy. Whatever cologne he wore, he smelled good, too good. Kelsey inched back in her chair until she could go no farther. She didn't need a Ph.D. to know Will Addison was trouble. Big trouble. "This year."

"But today's the thirty-first of January. That's only…"

"Two weeks away. It's short notice, but—"

"Sorry, not possible." With little regret, she closed the planner. It would be much better this way. Much better for her, that was.

"You have another wedding scheduled?"

Kelsey hesitated. This wasn't her problem, her fault. Yet the intense look on his face... "I did, but it was canceled after the bride met someone else."

The edges of his mouth turned up slightly. "So you can coordinate my sister's wedding."

She noticed he wasn't asking her a question. "I can't. Several clients offered to move their weddings up to Valentine's Day, but I decided to take advantage of the cancellation and give my staff a well-deserved vacation. Everyone's gone."

Hope brightened his eyes, making them sparkle like emeralds. Not jewels, Kelsey told herself, but broccoli or AstroTurf or anything else that would be green and unromantic. Remember he's married. And even if he wasn't... "You're here," he said.

"Not for long. My flight leaves in three hours." Kelsey reached for a nearby pad of paper and a pen. "I can give you some names of other wedding designers, but at this late date—"

"You don't understand." He brushed his hand through his hair, giving it an even more careless look than before. "It has to be you."

"May I ask why?"

"Both my mother and my sister want it to be you."

The desperation in Will's voice almost made her believe it was true. He was a good actor, real good. "If it's so important to them, why didn't they come?"

His lips tightened, and he glanced at the pile of magazines. "It's...complicated."

It always was. "Mr. Addison, I'm about to leave the country for a much-needed vacation. I don't have time for complications."

He stared directly into her eyes, and Kelsey felt woozy. "My sister is Faith Starr."

Of all the nerve... Kelsey's blood pressure soared off the chart and perspiration wet the back of her neck. "Faith Starr?"

At least Kelsey now knew why Will Addison's name sounded familiar—he was a blood relation, a brother no less, of the world's worst client. It was all coming back to her. Will was the oldest of the siblings who traveled the globe running the family chain of Starr Properties—resorts, hotels and inns named for his mother—that catered to the rich, famous and not-so-famous. Just as Starr Addison's husband, Bill, had used his wife's name for the family's real-estate venture, Faith had taken her mother's name for her stage name. Not that it made a difference.

Nothing made a difference where Faith Starr was concerned.

Kelsey rose, barely able to contain the anger threatening to erupt worse than Mt. Vesuvius. She was an Armstrong and had been raised properly to follow etiquette and protocol, but one could only be polite for so long. "Get out of my office, Mr. Addison. Now."

He stood. "I understand why you're upset. Faith hasn't been the most reliable—"

"Your sister is nothing more than a spoiled starlet, who strings fiancés along as if they were her personal puppets." Faith Starr, actress extraordinaire and the world's most famous runaway bride, had almost given Kelsey an ulcer—four times in the past three years. Faith was a perfectionist both in her craft and in planning her weddings. Never had Kelsey worked so hard with so little payoff in her life.

"I've already planned four weddings for her. Count

them—four." Kelsey raised four fingers. That was three too many. More business was one thing, but this... "I won't be involved in number five."

"Can't we talk about this? Work something—"

"Out. I have nothing more to say on this matter so please leave."

"If you only understood the circumstances—"

"Look," Kelsey said, trying to keep her tone polite, yet firm. "I appreciate you came on behalf of your family. That's very...noble of you considering my past with your sister. But nothing you say will change my mind."

His assessing gaze made her self-conscious. It was all she could do not to smooth her skirt and check to see if a piece of spinach was caught between her teeth. "Are you always so stubborn?" he asked, his eyes twinkling.

"Out. Now." At least the band of gold wasn't the only negative thing about Will Addison. "Get out of my office before I call security and have you thrown out."

Waiting for Kelsey to step out into the hallway was far from Will's idea of a good time, but he wasn't leaving until he had a chance to speak with her again.

The seconds turned into minutes; the minutes into an hour. How much longer before she left for the airport? He stared at the door to Kelsey's office. No catchy name for her business, simply Kelsey Armstrong Waters, Wedding Consultant, in a script font. Too bad there was nothing simple about the woman herself.

He should have handled it better, but Kelsey had caught him off guard, and he wasn't a man used to being caught off guard. He didn't like the feeling one bit.

Damn Faith.

Will was going to kill her. He shouldn't have promised to oversee her wedding planning while she finished filming her latest movie. Faith had said this would be easy. As easy as pushing an elephant into an elevator. And the wedding was the least of it.

Will was used to being around beautiful, wealthy, accomplished women and having them flirt, even pursue him. He was used to tolerating such women; he was an expert at fending off their advances unless he wanted a little company. But it never went further than that. No one intrigued him enough to make him want more.

Until today.

Something had happened when he'd seen Kelsey's reflection in the mirror. He'd stood transfixed as if watching a piece of living art. Unguarded expressions had played on her face, and emotion clogged his throat. He'd felt as if he were trespassing, but he hadn't been able to stop staring at her. Tall and willowy, with long chestnut hair that shone and sparkled as if each strand had been individually cleaned and polished, she looked so young, so soft, so sweet. The wistful smile on her face had touched his heart and he'd wanted to capture the moment. For the first time in a long while, he'd felt the racing of his pulse, the pounding of his heart. And he'd liked the way it felt. Liked it a lot.

When Kelsey had realized she wasn't alone, the glowing bride-to-be had metamorphosed into the cool, distant professional. No flirting, no fawning. She'd even called him "Mr. Addison" and kept it strictly business.

Yet when she'd realized he was Faith Starr's brother... Talk about passion boiling under a cool facade. Will couldn't believe the change in the woman. Flames had danced within the violet depths of her eyes, raising his temperature enough to melt the ice in his veins. She'd shown restraint, yet her anger had been clear. No amount of charm would ever change her mind. Forget the sweet talk, even his never-fail smile hadn't worked.

Will didn't get it. He always got what he wanted from women. Even with Sara.

Sara.

Will's gut tightened.

What the hell was he doing? Being attracted to Kelsey was one thing. He hadn't spent the past eight years as a total hermit, but he had no right to be intrigued by her. She wasn't simply a guest at one of his resorts; she was the woman he had to convince to plan his sister's wedding. His family, most especially his mother, was counting on him to bring Kelsey to Lake Tahoe. He wouldn't let his mother down. He couldn't let her down.

The door to Kelsey's office finally opened. She stepped out, locked the door and turned. The moment she saw him, her lips tightened. "What are you still doing here?"

Her above-the-knee gray tailored suit hugged each and every curve. Will forced his gaze to focus off her body and on her face. There was both a delicacy and a strength to her features. Her classic beauty would only improve over the years, and she didn't need all that makeup. High cheekbones dusted with blush, full lips painted the color of a mouthwatering plum and eyelids outlined with black liner. At least she hadn't tried to hide the small mole near the left side of her mouth. "You seemed upset. I wanted to apologize."

She stared down her perfectly shaped nose as if he were a mere peon. Fine by him. Will knew how to deal with women like that. He made a living catering to customers, to the whims of the wealthy guests staying at his family's resorts. He hadn't thought Kelsey fit that cold and shallow mold. She'd seemed more the warm and passionate type, but it would be easier this way. Much easier. "I also wanted to apologize for Faith. She's very sorry for what she put you through."

"Which time?"

"All four of them," he admitted.

Unblinking, Kelsey studied him. "You've said your apologies, now leave."

"I don't blame you for being upset at Faith, but I wish you would hear me out. You didn't lose money on any of her weddings."

"No, your mother saw to that, but I lost something far more valuable—my time." Kelsey flipped her hair behind her shoulder, and Will felt a twinge in his groin. Ignore it; ignore her. She continued, "And it hurt my reputation. In a business like this, reputation is everything."

"Granted, but Faith has changed. She loves her new fiancé and is serious about getting married this time."

"Which of her latest co-stars is she engaged to?"

"He isn't an actor."

The news seemed to surprise Kelsey, but she continued to stare at the gilt-framed botanical print on the wall. "A director, then?"

"No. His name is Trent Jeffreys. He runs a nonprofit agency."

"Nonprofit?"

"Low-cost housing, affordable living alternatives. He's even got Faith volunteering on a few of his projects."

"So he's not in the business." From the prim tone of her voice, Will could tell Kelsey still wasn't swayed.

"I don't think having a two-week engagement shows any growth on Faith's part."

He saw her point. "She's been engaged since Halloween."

"So why are you only coming to me now?"

Here's where it got tricky, Will realized. Once Kelsey agreed to come with him, she'd learn the truth, but for now that was family business and private. Will wished he could keep it that way, too. Thinking about what had happened to his mother was hard enough. He didn't want to talk about it. Might as well dangle the big carrot instead to see if Kelsey bit.

"As I said, it's the real deal this time. No more Hollywood extravaganzas like the weddings Faith asked you to plan for her. She and Trent want a small wedding with only close friends and family in attendance."

"Doesn't matter. At this late date every place is booked for Valentine's Day."

"Not the Starr Lake Inn at Tahoe."

Kelsey's sharp gaze met his. "Weddings aren't allowed at Starr Properties."

"True. They are intrusive on our other guests, but rules are made to be broken. Especially for family." Will saw he'd piqued her interest. "Unfortunately, the plans for Faith's wedding have gotten—how should I put it?—a little out of hand. We aren't known for putting on weddings, and we need a professional like yourself to help us with the finishing touches and the final arrangements."

Kelsey said nothing. The seconds ticked by. Time to seal the deal. America knew how wealthy the Armstrong family was, so money wouldn't be a good motivator. But according to his mother, Kelsey's business meant the world to her. "If you agree to work on Faith's wedding, we'll allow you to use a Starr property for a future wedding. Any wedding.''

Kelsey's eyes widened. Yes, her interest was genuinely piqued. Leave it to his mother...

"I'd want an exclusive contract to use any Starr property.''

Will was used to negotiating with cutthroat Realtors, city planners, you name it. Sharks, all of them. Kelsey was as sharp and smart. And something told him he would enjoy the challenge. Will smiled. "Only one?''

"At least one at each of your properties.''

Ouch. The shark bit off one of his limbs and spit it back at him. She reminded him of his mother. Starr was the reason the resorts were such a success. She had taught him everything she knew about business and negotiating. His mother had also taught him when to cut bait. "Fine. You may put on one wedding at each property provided you work with my office and use our chefs and staff.''

Kelsey got a faraway look in her eyes and it softened the features on her face, reminding him of how she'd looked when he'd first stepped inside her office and saw her in the veil. "Let me get this straight. All I have to do to get this wonderful opportunity is cancel my vacation, go with you to Lake Tahoe for the next two weeks and work on Faith's wedding?''

"Yes.''

"I don't think so.''

He did a double take. "What did you say?''

"I said no.'' She adjusted the leather bag on her shoulder. "Not even the exclusive use of Starr properties could make me want to work with your sister again. Now, if you'll excuse me, I have a plane to catch.'' Kelsey pushed past him.

Her strength of will impressed him. At least she had principles. But everyone had a price. He only had to find hers. "What would change your mind?"

She pursed her lips. "Do you have another sister who wants to get married?"

"Hope's already married."

"Sorry."

But he could tell she wasn't. Damn. He'd never expected her to turn down his offer... Now he was in a real bind, which left him only one other option.

To tell her the truth. "Wait."

She turned. "What is it now?"

"There's something I haven't told you about why we need you to plan Faith's wedding."

"That doesn't surprise me."

This was hard. Much harder than he thought it would be. Will tugged on his now-too-tight collar. "My mother was the one coordinating and making all the plans."

"Then you don't need me. Starr's amazing. She could plan any event with her eyes closed."

Kelsey was right on the mark about his mother. Starr Addison could do anything she put her mind to, except the one thing that had become her all-consuming goal— marry off her youngest daughter. "That was before," he forced the words out.

"Before what?"

"My mother had a stroke, and she..." Swallowing hard, he pulled himself together. "She said the only one she trusted to pull off the wedding she'd planned for Faith is you."

Chapter Two

Starr? A stroke?

It wasn't possible. But the seriousness in Will's gaze told Kelsey it was true. Tears stung her eyes and she blinked them away. "How is she doing?"

He shrugged, his features tight. "Things are progressing…slowly."

A stroke. Kelsey didn't know what to say. She remembered the helpless feeling that had engulfed her and her entire family when her grandmother Waters had suffered a stroke. The long days and endless nights until Grandmother had had another stroke and died. Kelsey fought the urge to offer comfort. He had a wife to do that. "I'm so sorry. I truly am."

"Thanks." His voice was deeper than she'd heard before, and he glanced at the ceiling. "It's been a…difficult time for all of us. Faith wanted to postpone the wedding, but my mother insists it goes on as planned. Mom wanted to continue doing all the work herself, but it was too much for her."

Too much for Starr Addison? Kelsey tried to imagine Starr as anything other than her vibrant and energetic self, a woman who'd even tried snowboarding last year just to see what it was like. A strong, confident woman who still had an Achilles' heel—her daughter, Faith.

Each time Faith decided at the eleventh hour to cancel her wedding, Starr would break the news to Kelsey and hand her a generous check for the work she'd done as if money would wipe the slate clean. Starr apologized for the inconvenience, but not once had she apologized for her daughter's actions. Neither had Faith, for that matter. Kelsey chalked it up to family loyalty. Still, a simple "I'm sorry" would have made such a difference, but none had come.

She'd kept waiting and hoping. Of course, she'd only contributed to the situation by continuing to plan Faith's weddings, because Kelsey enjoyed working with Starr, but she wasn't going to give in and do it again.

Kelsey really wanted—no, she *needed* to take a vacation. Just her reaction to Will told her she needed to get away from her daily routine. Designing wedding after wedding without time for herself or a little male diversion had taken a toll. A couple of weeks on the island paradise of San Montico with her cousin, Christina, was exactly what Kelsey needed. A little rest and relaxation. Maybe Prince Richard's royal advisor, Didier Alois, had forgiven her for turning down his marriage proposal and they could spend some time together. If he hadn't, making up would be a nice challenge. She did enjoy his company even if he'd gone a bit far by proposing after only knowing her for one week. And a casual flirtation might be fun. Yes, this vacation was what she needed, craved, deserved. "I'm really sorry, Will, but I have a plane to catch."

"My mother's only wish is to see Faith married. It's more important to her than her own recovery." He gazed straight at Kelsey, making her feel as if she needed to take a step—make that ten steps—back. "And you're the only one she wants to help her."

An invisible noose tightened around Kelsey's neck, and she tried to resist caving in. The last thing in the world she wanted to do was to plan a fifth wedding for Faith. Kelsey had promised herself not to allow Starr to sweet-talk her into doing another wedding for her daughter. Now it wasn't only Starr asking, but Will, too.

"What do you say?" He shifted his weight from one foot to the other. "Will you help my mother make her dream come true?"

A grapefruit-size lump of guilt lodged in Kelsey's throat. Closing her eyes, she thought about her grandmother and how important dreams had been to her. Dreams she'd had for and shared with each of her grandchildren. But the stroke had taken away those dreams, taken away everything. There had been little time to do anything but say goodbye. Kelsey had wanted to do more, so much more. And now Will was giving her the chance she hadn't had before.

The ding of a bell announced the arrival of the elevator, and the doors opened.

"I know your staff is gone, but I'll help you." Will smiled. "Tell me what you need done and it'll be done. I don't know much about weddings, but I'm a fast learner."

Her eyes sprang open and her heart leaped with pleasure at the thought of being near Will. It was totally illogical, downright ridiculous. Forget about not wanting to work on Faith's wedding. The last thing in the world Kelsey wanted to do was to spend two weeks working with Will Addison. "Faith will want to work on her own wedding."

"She's on location and won't be flying in until the day before the wedding. She made me promise to oversee things until she arrived."

This didn't sound like the Faith that Kelsey knew. The starlet wanted to be involved with everything. She'd even overseen the flower arrangements for the last wedding. Starr was always a big help, but even she demurred to her daughter's wishes. "Faith trusts you to oversee her wedding preparations?"

"Yes." A wry grin graced his lips. "Do you have a problem with this?"

Kelsey's stomach twisted and turned and tumbled. She should have eaten more than a croissant for breakfast. "Of course not. I've worked with grooms—men—before."

"Does this mean you'll do it?"

"I..." Glancing at the closing elevator doors ahead of her, she watched her vacation disappear. And with it, her stress level inched upward.

"You can't imagine what it would mean to my mother and my entire family."

Damn him. Damn all the Addisons. She did not want to work on another wedding for Faith. Kelsey had promised herself she wouldn't, yet for her grandmother and Starr... "Okay."

"Okay what?"

"I'll coordinate Faith's wedding." The gruffness of Kelsey's voice should have bothered her, but it didn't. She was doing this under duress. "I'm not saying it again."

"I'm not asking you to." Will grinned. He was practically dancing like a bride-to-be registering at Tiffany & Co.

At least one of them was getting some enjoyment out of this. She knew it wouldn't be her. She wouldn't be happy until February fifteenth—when Faith's wedding was over and done with, and Kelsey was back home. "I want an exclusive contract to plan weddings at Starr Properties. As many weddings as I want."

"Fine."

"And my normal fee went up." Money didn't mean much to her, but she wanted to make them pay. This seemed as good a way as any. Unlocking the door to her office, Kelsey stepped inside. "Way up."

He followed her in. "Okay."

"I need to pack a few things here. I'll also have to stop by my condo, repack my suitcase and make a few phone calls." She paused, wondering if she could make him change his mind about taking her with him. Not the fairest way to play, but she was desperate. "It'll take a little while. I understand if you don't want to wait."

"I'm happy to wait."

Anything to make her happy, Kelsey realized. She was tempted to ask him to jump to see if he would. She set her bag on the reception desk instead. With no warning, Will touched her shoulder, sending shivery sensations shooting up and down the length of her arm. "You don't know how much this means to me."

"Let's get one thing clear." She moved away from him, from his much-too-pleasurable touch. She'd brushed off advances from a few of the most handsome actors and musicians in the business—some even grooms-to-be. That had been bad enough, but this was much worse. Will was already married. M-a-r-r-i-e-d.

"I'm not doing this for you. I'm doing it for your mother."

And my grandmother.

"I understand."

Kelsey shook her finger at him. "And I swear if Faith doesn't get married this time..."

"I know my sister." He smiled. "She's getting married on February fourteenth."

Kelsey flashed him one of her give-me-a-break looks. "Care to make a wager on it?"

His eyes gleamed as if amused by the idea. "It's a sucker's bet."

"I happen to like suckers." She grinned. "Lime's my favorite."

"Cherry happens to be mine."

"So I'm tart and you're sweet." She laughed. "This could make for an interesting wager."

He smiled. "Seriously, there's no need for us to bet. Faith will go through with it this time. Trent's different than her other fiancés. What you see is what you get. No games, no ego trips. Faith's found the one."

"The one?" Kelsey tried not to sound too incredulous.

"Her soul mate, heart mate, love of a lifetime."

Surely he couldn't be serious. Yet the wistful look in his eyes was hard to ignore. Of course, it must be the lighting. Men weren't wistful about such things. Especially married men. Yet a part of her wondered if Will had married what he believed to be his "one." Kelsey tucked a strand of hair behind her ear. "Don't tell me *you* believe in those things?"

"Of course I do." His eyes narrowed. "Just because I'm a guy doesn't mean I'm not..."

"A romantic at heart?" she offered.

He nodded. "There's nothing wrong with being romantic. Women like that in a man."

Kelsey shrugged. "Some women might, others..."

"I feel sorry for those who don't."

Oh, boy, they came in all shapes and sizes, those romantic idealists who believed in love at first sight and happily-ever-after, but she'd never met one in a more perfect package than Will Addison. Too bad she didn't share any of his beliefs. No, it wasn't too bad. After everything she'd been through growing up, Kelsey knew better. That should kill whatever attraction she felt for Mr. Romance.

She headed toward the storage room. "Would you give me a hand?"

Together they carried the leather trunk she took with her on out-of-town weddings into the office. From Telluride to Turkey, the contents of the trunk had saved the day more than once.

Will tapped the top of the trunk. "What's this for?"

"Anything I might need to keep me from having to run around a town I'm not familiar with and waste time I don't have to spare. You'd be amazed at what can happen the morning of a wedding."

She opened the trunk, rummaged through it and made a mental list of what needed to be packed. "Does Faith have a wedding dress to wear?"

"Yes."

"That's right. I forgot," Kelsey said. "She's got four of them. Let's hope she hasn't had any alterations done yet, in case she's a no-show again."

Will laughed. At least he had a sense of humor. Not that it mattered, she reminded herself.

"Does she have a headpiece and veil?"

The smile faded from his face. "My mother planned

to make one herself à la Martha Stewart. She got hooked on crafting last summer, but the stroke…''

"I've got plenty to choose from." Kelsey stared at her selection. "Do you know what style of gown Faith's chosen?"

"No," Will admitted. "That's been the most highly guarded secret, next to her engagement itself."

"Not a problem." Kelsey packed a variety of head-pieces—halos, silk flower wreaths, beaded tiaras and different-length veils—in the trunk. If worse came to worst, she'd call in a few favors owed her. "We'll bring several with us."

"What about the one you were wearing?"

It would kill her to let Faith wear the vintage ensemble, but even Kelsey had to admit it would look lovely with the movie star's long wavy locks. "I'll pack it."

"Do you need anything else in here?"

She gathered up a couple of garters and guest books in case Starr hadn't gotten around to that, either. "Would you grab the lavender toolbox in the storage room?"

"A toolbox?"

"Tricks of the trade." And right now she needed every trick she had up her sleeve to get through packing her gear with Will's help. If it felt strange here in her own office, she didn't want to think about what it would be like working with him in Lake Tahoe.

"What tricks would those be?"

"Sewing needles, thread, safety pins, first-aid kit, clear nail polish, hair spray, things like that."

"You're very prepared."

"I have to be," she admitted. "My clients expect nothing less. I do my best to make sure their wedding day is the most perfect, the happiest day of their lives."

He stared at her with an odd look on his face. "A person's wedding day is only the first of many happy days."

Using all of her willpower, she managed not to roll her eyes. "Wasn't your wedding day your happiest day ever?"

Her question seemed to catch him off guard, but only for a moment. The sweet smile on his face made Kelsey swallow hard and remind herself he was already taken. "Yes, it was the best day of my life."

The dreamy tone of his voice touched a place deep within her heart. His wife was a lucky woman. Or would be until the marriage started unraveling and falling apart... No doubt they hadn't been married long or faced any bumps in the matrimony road. "Told you so. Every bride and groom deserve a perfect wedding day, even your sister."

Will stared at Kelsey. "You take what you do very seriously."

"If I didn't, I wouldn't be doing it."

"So you're a romantic at heart, too?"

"I wouldn't go that far." She smiled at the ridiculous notion. No one she knew would ever call her romantic. "I'm more of a...realist."

A realist, she thought, who knew the truth—there was no such thing as "happily ever after."

Sitting in the living room of Kelsey's condo in Brentwood, Will tried to make sense of the woman who'd agreed to coordinate Faith's wedding. Kelsey hadn't said yes out of the goodness of her heart. She would be well paid and receive an exclusive contract to put on weddings at Starr Properties. But he'd seen her genuine concern over his mother's condition. The tears in Kelsey's eyes, the slight quiver of her lower lip, the cracking of her voice.

From the doorway of what Will assumed was Kelsey's bedroom, she leaned out, a toiletry bag in one hand, a cordless phone in the other. "I'm going to be a few more minutes. Would you like something to drink?"

"I'm fine, thanks."

Watching her pack a trunk of wedding paraphernalia in her office had been like watching Tiger Woods play golf. Not one motion wasted, not one hit bunker. Here, she was no different and made multitasking look as effortless as a stroll through the park on a spring morning. "Do you need any help?"

"No, thanks."

This didn't surprise him. He'd never seen a more self-sufficient, organized woman before. No wonder his mother had been so adamant about his bringing her back with him. "Let me know if you do."

"Okay." With that she was gone.

Strictly business. Minimal exchanges. Polite manners. That's how Kelsey had been for the past hour. He should be pleased. Yet, Will couldn't forget the look of pure joy on her face when she'd tried on the veil or the flirtatious smile and the way she'd batted her eyelashes when she'd first seen him. She was a contradiction. That much he'd discovered in the short time they'd known each other.

Will settled back on the couch. Obviously there was more to Kelsey than met the eye. Professional and smooth on the outside, he could only wonder what was going on in the inside.

He was very good at reading people. Over the years he'd learned to anticipate the needs and wants of his guests as his mother had when she'd convinced his father to buy the Lake Inn so many years ago. That's what made Starr Properties so successful. But Will was having trouble figuring out Kelsey. Dressed in her designer clothes with perfectly applied makeup and just the right amount of jewelry and accessories, she might look like one of his clients, she may have even been one. But she wasn't the norm.

Not by a long shot.

And that's what bothered him. He wanted her to be like the norm. He wanted her to look ordinary, not stand out. He didn't want to notice her. He didn't want her to be different or unique. He couldn't afford the distraction or any entanglements. Regardless of his attraction, or whatever it was, to Kelsey, Will had to concentrate on Faith's wedding. That's what really mattered.

In two weeks his sister would be married, his mother would be happy and the intriguing wedding consultant would be out of his life. Two weeks. Only fourteen days. He'd make it. He'd survive as he always did.

Will stared at the pictures covering the walls and on the fireplace mantel. Most were photographs of the Armstrong family. Politicians, lawyers, doctors and corporate elite. Darlings of the paparazzi and one of the closest things to royalty America had. The most recent photo—resembling a family reunion with numerous aunts, uncles and cousins—had been taken in front of the San Montico royal palace. Last summer's royal wedding had been the social event of the year and broadcast live all over the globe. His mother had gushed over the fairy-tale romance and asked Will to watch the wedding with her. He'd passed. Much to her regret then, and his now.

Losing Sara had made him realize how important his

family was, but he still had taken his parents' and sisters' love for granted. No longer, which was one reason he was here.

Kelsey reappeared in the doorway. "If you're bored, there are magazines in the ottoman. I'll be ready in a few minutes."

Before he could say anything, she disappeared. Will opened the ottoman that doubled as a coffee table. Inside were stacks of magazines ranging from *Bride* to *Vanity Fair,* a few of the latest bestselling novels and a couple of photo albums.

Curious, Will removed one of the albums. Opening the cover, he saw it was more a scrapbook than a photo album. It contained everything from actual wedding pictures to newspaper and magazine clippings about various weddings.

As Will flipped through the pages, he recognized the extent of her clientele. But something else happened, too. A soothing warmth filled him. Kelsey had surprised him yet again. Realist or not, someone who put this much time and effort into preserving the memory of each wedding she coordinated had to be sentimental.

Each two-page spread contained photographs of the bride and groom and the reception and keepsakes from the wedding such as a ribbon or ceremony program. Everything was neatly matted on coordinating paper and she'd written captions under each item.

He continued paging through the book. Each wedding was different. From movie stars to political figures, Kelsey had managed to pull off spectacular and unique weddings for each of them. Some were enormous affairs with media coverage and security, but others appeared to be more intimate gatherings. That made him happy since that's what his family was hoping for.

After he reached the end and put the album back in the ottoman, a satisfied smile formed on his lips. Taking Kelsey home was the right move. Someone so warm and fuzzy was what they all needed—correction, what his mother needed. And Faith, too.

Opening the next scrapbook, he expected to see more wedding memorabilia. He didn't. Will turned one page, then another, and another. This book didn't celebrate her clients' marriages, but their divorces.

Will frowned. He couldn't believe what he was reading. Page upon page of clippings. Ugly accusations, tearful confessions, angry photographs. Her clientele was the kind to get as much press coverage with their divorces as with their weddings. In the upper corner of each page Kelsey had noted the years, sometimes only days, the marriage lasted. Will tried to reconcile the first book with the second. He couldn't.

The first book showed how much she loved her job and the photographs and clippings reaffirmed her talent for designing weddings, but the second scrapbook was the exact opposite. He didn't get it. Something didn't add up. He placed the book in the ottoman and closed the lid.

Kelsey entered the room with one suitcase in her hand, another rolling behind her, and a bag on her shoulder. "I'm ready now."

Will hesitated. Should he mention the scrapbooks? He was supposed to bring her home with him, but was it in his family's best interest to put her in charge of Faith's wedding? Now he wondered, after what he'd just seen. The divorce album rubbed him the wrong way, made him wonder if Kelsey had a hidden agenda or something. He felt as if he'd opened the cupboard of a health fanatic only to find a stash of junk food.

"Is something wrong?" she asked.

A perfect segue, but something held him back. Was he reading too much into this? Maybe the divorce album was some kind of joke. Maybe he was too embarrassed to admit he'd peeked at her scrapbooks. Maybe he was looking for any excuse not to take her home with him and spend the next two weeks by her side.

"No." His goal had been to get Kelsey to coordinate the wedding. It's what his mother wanted. It's what Faith had asked him to do. No sense changing course now despite his own reservations. Will rose from the couch. "Let's go. Our plane is waiting for us."

Talk about a bumpy flight. Another wave of turbulence shook the Learjet. Kelsey checked her seat belt for the zillionth time. Habit, she realized. Turbulence, she could handle. But Will Addison?

No matter which way she turned, she could see him, smell him, sense him. Talk about feeling claustrophobic. If only she had a parachute...

Kelsey didn't understand what was going on. Okay, that wasn't the entire truth. But the truth bothered her, made her feel lower than low. Not even worthy of being on the bottom of the food chain. Will might be Faith's brother; he might even be married. But Kelsey was attracted to him, attracted to his looks and his smile and his easygoing manner.

And she hated herself for the way she felt.

She sunk into the luxurious leather seat and leaned her head back. Married might as well mean leprosy because in her book Will was untouchable, off limits, you name it. She would not be a catalyst to the breakup of a marriage. Kelsey would sooner gouge out her eyes than get involved with a married man. Which meant she had to ignore her attraction for Will Addison, had to ignore he was even a man.

She knew exactly what infidelity could do to a marriage, to a family. Her father had been the first to stray, but her mother had followed in his footsteps until all hell had broken loose. The accusations, the fighting, the tears. She and her brother, Cade, had been the ones to lose, the ones turned into pawns in a vicious winner-take-all custody battle.

Will shifted in his seat and stretched his long legs out in front of him. His calf brushed hers and a burst of heat emanated from the point of contact.

Ignore it, she ordered herself. Something told her she would be having to ignore many things over the next two weeks.

"So how did you become a wedding consultant?" he asked.

Thank goodness. A safe topic. Business related even. Kelsey counted her lucky stars. "My parents divorced when I was nine. When it came time for them to marry others, they both asked for my brother's and my input. I think it was their way of trying to make things easier on us. My brother couldn't have cared less, but I got into it. Each time they remarried—"

"Each time?"

"My father's been married eight times, my mother six, though she's currently engaged to number seven," Kelsey admitted. It wasn't a big secret to anyone who knew anything about the Armstrongs. Many followed the happenings of America's second most famous family. "Needless to say, I had lots of practice planning weddings."

"How did you pick Beverly Hills to open your business?"

"When I was thirteen, my mother married a producer, who moved us from Chicago to Beverly Hills and introduced me to the entertainment industry. He's husband number three and five."

Will's eyes widened. "She married him twice?"

Kelsey nodded. "And divorced him twice, too."

Will frowned. "Your family sounds a lot different than mine."

"I know. Your parents have been together forever. Starr was very proud about that."

Will smiled. "Divorce is a four-letter word in our house. No Addison has ever been divorced."

"None of them?"

"No grandparents, aunts, uncles, cousins or siblings."

"That's...unbelievable."

"But true." Pride rang out in his voice, and Kelsey felt a stab of envy. "We've all been fortunate to find the right person."

"Not Faith."

"She hasn't married yet."

"You don't have to remind me." Kelsey stared at him. "So, do Addisons stay in miserable marriages to avoid divorce?"

"We don't have miserable marriages."

And there was a pot of gold at the end of every rainbow. "Seems to me most marriages end up that way eventually, unless you are lucky."

He raised a brow. "This from a wedding consultant?"

She nodded. "That's why I take my job so seriously. Every bride deserves to feel like a princess and every groom a prince. The least I can do is give a couple a day to remember, a day to hold close to their hearts after things sour.''

''Is that why you keep a scrapbook of your clients' divorces? Not one showing the successful marriages, the pictures of babies and children that come from the ones that work?''

A mixture of embarrassment and anger washed over her, yet she contained her temper. Like it or not, Will was a client. And as she'd learned from her parents, blowing up over something that couldn't be changed never solved anything. She shrugged, but the last thing she felt was indifference. No one had ever seen her scrapbooks. Until that moment she'd forgotten she'd put them in the ottoman instead of their usual hiding place. ''Not many of the marriages I coordinate last.''

''No doubt because of your Wedding Consultant to the Stars moniker.'' Sarcasm laced his voice. ''You haven't seen what real marriages are all about, how good, how strong they can be.''

''Is that how you feel about your marriage?''

''Yes.''

She'd seen too many failed marriages to believe the Addisons had the market cornered on happy ones. ''You think you found your soul mate?''

''I have no doubt.''

Kelsey heard the conviction in his voice. Such a romantic. She couldn't ignore her curiosity about his wife, the woman who'd captured Will Addison's heart. ''How did you know she was the 'one'?''

He got a faraway look in his eyes. ''It happened the day I met her.''

Love at first sight? Talk about a fairy tale. This she had to hear. ''How did you meet?''

Will glanced out the window to the red-streaked sky.

The sun was setting slowly. "It was Sadie Hawkin's day. I was in sixth grade. All the boys tied their names on their belt loops and the girls got to chase us. If a girl managed to get your name, you were hers for the day."

He and his wife had been childhood sweethearts and still together after all this time. Kelsey found that hard to believe in this day and age. "Sounds...fun."

"For the girls maybe," he admitted. "Sara, my wife, was new to the school. I'd never really paid much attention to her before because she was so shy and quiet..." His voice trailed off.

"Go on."

He hesitated. "Sometime during the chase, one of the girls pushed her. Sara fell. Her knee was bloody and she was crying. I went over to help her up."

"Don't tell me she grabbed your name tag?"

He nodded.

"And that's how you knew?"

He moistened his lips. "Sara was holding on to my name and she smiled, a wide grin with a mouthful of braces, and I knew."

"Knew what?"

"That one day I would marry her." He glanced away. "And I did. Two days after I graduated from college. That was ten years ago."

"You were young."

"I wish I'd married her sooner."

"That's sweet." Saccharine sweet, Kelsey thought. How could he feel that way after ten years? Longer if one counted how long they'd been together. Maybe he'd gotten lucky, like his parents and grandparents.

His eyes glimmered. Tears? Kelsey found that almost as hard to believe as being married forever. Maybe he

MELISSA McCLONE   43

wore contacts and had a piece of grit in one of his eyes. That would explain it.

"I'm looking forward to meeting her," Kelsey said to break the silence.

"You can't meet her." The green of Will's eyes darkened and his lips tightened. "Sara...is dead. She was killed in a car crash eight years ago."

Chapter Three

The air whooshed from Kelsey's lungs. Talk about
open-foot-insert-mouth. She struggled for a breath and
the right—appropriate—words to say. Even though she
was able to handle even the most awkward situations,
this one left her speechless. Not wanting the uncomfortable silence to stretch any further, she settled for the
most obvious yet overused sentiment. "I'm so sorry,
Will."

"Thanks."

No pain in his voice; no anguish on his face, but that
didn't make her feel any better. Okay, his wife had died
eight years ago not eight days, but Kelsey still felt about
a quarter of an inch tall. It was obvious from everything
he'd said about love and marriage that his heart still
belonged to one woman and one woman only—his late
wife, Sara. "I hope I didn't—"

"You didn't."

"I thought since you wore a wedding band..."

"It's okay, Kelsey. Really."

She nodded, wanting to believe him and not wanting to say another word. Her brother would have a good laugh. Cade always called her Ms. Manners and teased her about writing an etiquette book when she tired of designing weddings. So much for handling any situation with aplomb and ease.

The muted whine of the plane's engine filled the cabin, kept the silence from becoming unbearable. Kelsey straightened in her seat and dug the toes of her black boots into the carpet. It couldn't be too much longer until they arrived at the airport. Yet each passing minute felt like an hour. She'd never heard Starr or Faith mention Will being a widower. They'd never even mentioned he'd been married. Questions about him filled Kelsey's mind. She wanted to know the answers, but she didn't dare ask.

Will looked to be in his early thirties. If Sara was his soul mate and one true love, did that mean he planned to spend the rest of his days alone? Kelsey wasn't sure whether his answer would make him the world's biggest romantic or the biggest fool. Surely he must have loved Sara—still loved her—if her memory was enough for him. Kelsey found it hard to believe anyone could love another that much.

Will cleared his throat. "Once we arrive, we'll head to the Lake Inn. You'll have the use of one of our suites."

"Thank you." The edges of Kelsey's mouth turned up slightly. "You were confident I'd come if you saved a room."

"Let's say I was hopeful," he admitted. "Tonight you can unpack and get settled in. We'll have breakfast at my parents' house and start work tomorrow."

She hesitated. This required the right amount of tact.

"I appreciate your offer to help, but I'm sure it would be a huge inconvenience to both you and Starr Properties to spend the next two weeks working with me."

He chuckled. "I appreciate your concern, but Starr Properties has been doing quite well these past few months without me working eighty hours a week. My staff knows how to find me if they need anything. And you know Faith. She'd kill me if I didn't keep her informed about everything you were doing. Trust me, it will be easier if I'm completely involved."

Easier for whom? Faith, sure. But what about her? Kelsey was beginning to think a free-fall descent onto a parking lot would be easier to survive than spending the next fourteen days with Will. Of course, she was simply overreacting.

Working with Will Addison wouldn't be difficult. So he was interesting? Charming and handsome, too? He was also a die-hard romantic. Kelsey wouldn't want to touch that with a ten-foot—make that a twenty-foot—pole. Not even a slight flirtation appealed to her. She settled back in her seat. These next two weeks were going to be a snap.

The drive from the airport to Lake Tahoe's North Shore passed without incident. It was dark by the time Will pulled his Yukon into the parking lot of the Starr Lake Inn.

Kelsey climbed out. Falling snowflakes greeted her and clung like confetti. Her breath hung in the chilly night air. She tugged the front of her jacket together.

As she faced the hotel, the sight warmed her. She almost thought she was in the Swiss Alps instead of the Sierra Nevadas. The charming inn with its horse-drawn sleigh waiting for passengers and its gingerbread-trimmed balconies on each of the floors was movie-facade perfect, but better than a set designer could fabricate on a sound stage because this was real.

She walked next to Will. A few yards from the lobby entrance, she noticed two men talking to a bellhop.

Kelsey froze. Every nerve ending went on alert. Garrett Malloy and Fred Silvers were reporters/photographers for *Weekly Secrets*, a cheesy tabloid that reported on celebrities with an almost-stalker-obsessive slant. If the dynamic duo caught sight of Kelsey and put two and two together, all bets for an intimate, private wedding would be off. She tried to stay out of sight. "We have a problem."

Will glanced back. "Only one?"

"No, two." Kelsey motioned to the men standing outside the entrance to the inn. "Sleazy tabloid reporters," she whispered. "They would kill for a scoop about Faith's wedding."

Will frowned. "I haven't told anyone except my personal assistant. There's no way they could have found out."

The two men walked toward them. A few more yards and they would see her. Kelsey couldn't take the chance. She glanced at Will. "Desperate times call for desperate measures."

Kelsey wrapped her arms around him and nuzzled her face against his neck. Warmth emanated from him. Even though he wore a jacket, she could feel how solid he was underneath. And boy, did he smell good. Even better close up. She took another sniff.

His sharp intake of air brought her back to reality. She shouldn't be enjoying this as much as she was. She shouldn't be enjoying this at all.

"What are you doing?" Tension filled his voice, made him stiffen.

"Hiding."

"You're only bringing attention to—"

"Just go with it," she whispered, "for Faith's sake."

Will blew out a puff of air. As the sound of footsteps crunching on the snow grew louder, he pulled Kelsey closer. And closer.

One of the reporters snickered.

This wasn't going to work. The reporters would recognize her. Put two and two together and...

Will covered her mouth with his own. Oh, my. The feel of his lips moving against hers made her close her eyes and moan. This was better than a kiss in a dream. Way better. Hot. Knee-melting hot. Soft. Purest cashmere soft. And delicious. Mouthwatering-soufflé delicious. She wanted more, so much more. Kelsey leaned into him, taking what she wanted.

"Get a room," a man—one of the reporters?—said.

Will deepened the kiss. The taste of him, the feel of him, the scent—all of it intoxicating. She could easily become addicted to this.

Before Kelsey knew what was happening Will stepped back and she nearly fell forward. She struggled to regain her composure, to make her heartbeat stop racing, to calm her ragged breathing.

"They're gone." He whipped out his cell phone and punched in a number as if the kiss hadn't had any effect on him.

And it hadn't, she realized. At least not on Will. But on her...

She might as well have just run the hundred-yard dash at the equator. Her blood boiled and her pulse raced and her heart pounded. Not even the cold night air managed to cool her down. Never before had she been kissed so thoroughly. And never before had she been so shaken.

Will closed his cell phone. "They haven't been the only reporters hanging around."

She struggled to forget about the kiss, forget about the ache building within her. "C-could your assistant—"

"No." His lips tightened. "Confidentiality is a priority at all Starr resorts. Besides, most people, including the guests, think we're throwing a thirty-fifth wedding anniversary party for my parents, not a wedding."

Kelsey did a double take. The kiss had muddied her mind, her senses. "An anniversary party?"

"My parents were married on Valentine's Day, too," Will explained. "My mother thought it would be romantic to have Faith marry on the same day as she and my father did."

The dash of romance was enough to clear Kelsey's head and force her to focus on the task at hand. Maybe sharing the same wedding date would be enough impetus for Faith to follow through this once. "At least it won't look odd for Faith to fly in for the anniversary party."

Will stared at Kelsey. "But it will look odd for you to be here."

Remember, the customer is always right. At least until you can get them to change their minds. Kelsey took a deep breath and exhaled slowly. "How am I supposed to coordinate a wedding without being on-site?"

"You can be on-site, but you'll have to keep a low profile. At least until the day of the event."

That she could handle. "A couple of weeks of room service won't be bad. I can work early in the mornings or late at night when the guests have retired to their rooms.''

Will furrowed his brow. "What about meeting with suppliers?"

"I'll manage," she said. "I've worked on top-secret weddings before."

"But the press still could find out."

"I'll stay at another hotel." She was used to last-minute changes. "If anyone asks why I'm here, I can say I'm scouting wedding sites. I'll rent a car and—"

"No." Will stared at her, his eyes cloudy. "You can stay with me."

"With you?"

"A path connects my house to the inn. It's a nice walk and you can enter and exit through the service entrance without being seen by the guests or the press. It's the only thing that makes sense."

Only if one were certifiable. "I don't want to impose."

"You won't," he said. "The press will get bored waiting for Faith to show up and then you can move into the inn. It'll be a few days at the most."

A few days. That didn't sound so bad to Kelsey as long as no more kisses were involved. And why in the world would they kiss again? "I'm sure it'll work out fine."

Fine. Her definition of the word and Will's had to be miles apart. The only way to make things work out fine was to get away from her—A.S.A.P. Will concentrated on his driving.

"Would you mind if I turned on the radio?" Kelsey asked.

"Go ahead." His voice sounded cool, even to him.

"There's a case of CDs between the seats if you'd rather listen to one of those."

She reached for the case. "Thanks."

So polite. Just an act, Will was certain. If she were truly polite, she wouldn't have kissed him back the way she had. The kiss had been nothing more than an act, and he wanted to pretend he hadn't felt anything. Pretend his space-shuttle-launch-explosive reaction hadn't been real. But it had. Will didn't like that, didn't like the way Kelsey had made him drop his guard if only for a few moments. There had been other women in his life since Sara's death, but not one a relationship he considered remotely serious. Nothing he couldn't forget or live without. Nothing he'd wanted to take to the next level.

But with Kelsey...

It had only been one kiss, but it had felt like coming home. Home to a place he'd forgotten existed after years of exile. He wanted to go back. Again and again.

And that made absolutely no sense.

Sara was the only one who had made him feel that way.

As Kelsey leaned forward to insert the CD in the player, he caught another tantalizing whiff of her perfume. The scent reminded him of her kiss. Passionate, seductive, hot. The perfume filled his nostrils the same way it had during the flight from L.A. Will tightened his grip on the steering wheel. He should have bought a Hummer instead. The front seats had to be farther apart than the ones in his Yukon. Who was he kidding? He could be sitting at the opposite end of a 747-400 and he'd still be able to smell her.

Her perfume, he corrected himself. Maybe she applied the scent with a heavy hand. Or maybe...

Don't go there.

And he didn't. Instead, Will searched the recesses of his memory. He glanced at his wedding band and struggled to remember the fragrance Sara had worn. Something light. Floral perhaps? Sweet and gentle as the woman herself. But he couldn't remember the scent, the name…nothing. What was happening to him? He should remember it, remember all of it.

"This is one of my favorites." Kelsey pushed Play. "I have it at home."

The sound of blues filled the confines of the truck. It was one of Will's favorite CDs, too, but right now anything would be better than music that brought smoky and sultry and seductive images to mind. He shifted in his seat. At least they didn't have far to drive.

Once again, he questioned what he was doing. Kiss or no kiss, taking her home with him was pure insanity. Eight bedrooms and six bathrooms aside. Unfortunately he hadn't had a choice. The words had been out of his mouth before he could stop them. An instinctive reaction. A way of changing what couldn't be changed.

I'll rent a car.

Those were the same words Sara had said to him over the telephone eight years ago. She had flown home from graduate school and arrived on time, but his flight from a business trip had been delayed. Not meeting him at the airport had dampened her spirits, but only for a moment. She was too excited about being finished with finals and spending an entire week with him. She offered to rent the car and leave his at the airport so he could make it home to her that much sooner. But a patch of black ice had changed everything. Ice had sent her car sliding into oncoming traffic. Ice had taken her young life and ruined his.

Feeling the familiar tightening of his heart, Will flicked on the right turn signal and turned off the emotion welling within him. He pulled into the long driveway and stopped in front of his house.

Only two weeks and Kelsey would be gone, he reminded himself. Gone.

Facing her, he pasted on his my-home-is-your-home resort owner smile. "Welcome to my home."

She stared at the house. "It's lovely. I expected to see a smaller version of the Starr inn, not a Victorian."

Across the wide expanse of the front porch, the golden hue of interior lights shining through the pane-glass windows emanated warmth. "My grandparents originally owned it, then gave it to my parents for a wedding present. My mom and dad turned it into a B and B. The humble beginnings of Starr Properties."

"You grew up in this house?"

"Yes. My parents had another house built a few years ago and, following tradition, passed the house down to the firstborn. Traditions are big in my family," he explained.

"I guessed as much." She smiled. "With all this snow, it looks like a winter wonderland. Something from a Thomas Kinkade painting. You know, it would be a charming site for a wedding."

"This one isn't part of our deal."

"I meant Faith's wedding. Imagine the bride and groom leaving in a horse-drawn sled."

"And you say you're not a romantic."

"I design weddings. By definition, weddings should be romantic. That doesn't mean I have to be."

One tough cookie. Will felt sorry for her. She didn't know what she was missing.

He slid out of the truck and removed Kelsey's bag

from the back. A breeze blew through the trees, sending more snow to the ground. Will walked next to Kelsey.

"Be careful." Snow covering the walkway crunched beneath his feet. "You don't want to slip."

"I won't slip." Confidence laced each of her words. He wouldn't have expected any less from her. "I've spent lots of time in cold-weather country."

He shortened his stride to match hers. Just in case. "Do you ski?"

"Excuse me?"

"You said you've spent time in cold-weather country. That usually means you ski or snowshoe or ice fish. You don't look like an ice-fishing enthusiast or snowshoer."

She wrinkled her nose. "I'm not. I ski."

"Cross-country or downhill?"

"Downhill. My family, the Armstrong side, spends part of the holidays skiing in Colorado. Every other year, my brother and I join them."

"And the other years?"

She pursed her lips. "We spend it with my father's side of the family."

"Have you skied recently?"

"To be honest, it's been a while. Work keeps me busy. People get married all year 'round."

"Thanks again for giving up your vacation to help us out."

She looked up at the dark sky. A snowflake landed on her mouth and she licked it off. "It feels good to be out of L.A."

He'd been in Los Angeles for less than a day, but he knew how she felt. "Fresh air is good for the soul."

"Anything has to be better than inhaling smog."

"Why do you stay?"

"It's home," she admitted. "You get used to the traffic, the air quality and the people after a while."

He could never get used to those things. Not when places like this existed. "You seem pretty normal for a SoCal resident."

She laughed. "I'll take that as a compliment."

"It was meant as one." Will took her elbow and helped her up the stairs.

"Thanks." Kelsey grinned. "Do you open doors and pull out chairs, too?"

"Always." He smiled. "My parents raised me right."

He opened the front door. She stepped inside and gasped. "Oh, Will. This is absolutely beautiful. I can picture it now. Faith could enter down the staircase for the wedding ceremony. We could drape the banister with a floral garland. Very old-fashioned. Victorian to match the house."

Will stared at her, trying to figure her out. He couldn't. "How do you do it?"

"Do what?"

"Picture exactly how a wedding will look. How beautiful, romantic, whatever, when you believe it'll make no difference in the long run?"

"It's a gift." Kelsey shrugged off her coat, and Will hung it on a coatrack. "Who do we have here?" she asked. Before Will could answer, she bent over and held her hand in front of Midas's nose, who sniffed her fingers. "You sure are a sweet kitty, aren't you? What's your name, handsome?"

"Midas," Will answered, not believing what he was seeing.

Midas meowed. He lapped up the attention and rubbed against her hand. Will's chest tightened. Most people kept there distance from Midas with only three legs and scars not even his long orange hair could disguise. Yet Kelsey picked Midas up and held him as if he were no different than any other cat. She hugged him close. Nuzzled him. And Midas ate it up. He loved to be cuddled more than anything.

"Listen to you purr," she said. "Any louder and you'd need a muffler."

Will laughed. "Why do you think we named him Midas?"

Kelsey grinned. "And to think I thought everything you touched turned to gold." She kissed the cat's forehead, then placed him on the hardwood floor. The orange fur ball rubbed against her calf and wouldn't leave her side.

Not that Will blamed him. There could much worse things in life than rubbing against those long legs of hers.

He raised his gaze to hers. She stared at him unwavering, as if she knew he was checking her out and was curious about his assessment. Nice package, he had to admit. Not that he was interested in said package, he told himself. If only the voice in his head would stop laughing, stop mocking him. "I'll show you to your room."

"Thanks."

He followed her up the stairs and tried to ignore the seductive sway of her hips. Everything about her oozed sensuality. It would be so easy to...

He couldn't.

Not with Kelsey. She was dangerous. Only a few hours in her presence had made his numb heart start feeling prickly, as if a million pins and needles were trying to bring to life something that had been dormant for much too long.

"Do you mind telling me what happened to Midas?"

"He was in a car accident. He survived. Sara... didn't."

"Oh, Will."

He stopped walking. Memories of that time always made it hard to for him to do more than one thing at a time. "At first I hated Midas for living. He was never my cat. Always Sara's. I kept thinking, Why couldn't he have died instead?"

Kelsey touched Will's arm. He ignored how good the small gesture felt, ignored how much he wanted, needed, to be touched. He concentrated on his cat and started walking down the hall.

"But watching him recover...it would have been easier on him if he hadn't survived." Will rubbed Midas. "He's on his sixth or seventh life by now."

Will opened the door to what used to be his sister Hope's room. Faith still considered her old room to be hers and would want to stay there when she arrived for the wedding. Hope, on the other hand, couldn't care less where she slept as long as her three children were within earshot. "Make yourself at home."

"Thanks." Kelsey placed her purse on the bed. "Like everything else in the house, it's perfect."

Her compliment brought a smile to his face. "I'll bring in your suitcase after I fix dinner."

"I'm not hungry, so don't go to any trouble."

"I won't."

His gaze met hers. He wanted to leave, but something held him in place. It was almost as if the distance between them wasn't empty space but a thick cord, connecting them. He hadn't felt this way since...

No, he'd had his chance at love.

He wouldn't get another one.

It wasn't so bad living alone. He had his family; he had his work. Children of his own would have been nice, but that hadn't been in the cards for him and Sara. But he had two nephews and a niece. Hope's kids. And once Faith married, she would have a few of her own. That was more than enough for him.

"I'll freshen up," Kelsey said, finally breaking the silence.

"I'll be downstairs when you're ready." He stopped at the doorway to call for Midas only to watch the cat follow Kelsey into the bathroom. "Traitor," he mumbled, feeling both betrayed and envious at the same time.

Chapter Four

February 1

Standing at the front door of Bill and Starr Addison's not-so-humble abode with Will at her side, Kelsey had one question running through her mind. How had she wound up here? The obvious answer was via Will's Yukon and, to take it a step further, by Will's plane. But the obvious wasn't what she was looking for.

Something was happening to her. And she didn't like it. This morning she'd woken up from the most strange yet sublime dream she'd ever had. A dream of fairy-tale weddings, magical kisses, enchanted bridal bouquets and a groom who bore a strong resemblance to Will Addison. No doubt wearing the veil yesterday had fueled her subconscious and the kiss they'd shared had stoked the fire, but it still made zero sense.

She wasn't the sort to remember dreams or even care about them, but she couldn't get this one—or Will—

out of her mind. What was happening to her? She never got carried away by this sort of stuff.

Okay, that wasn't completely true. Kelsey *had* gotten caught up in San Montico's Legend of the Ring when the royal engagement ring was stuck on her cousin Christina's finger. The legend claimed whoever wore the ring was the prince's one true love, and that's how it turned out. Christina had fallen in love and married the prince. But legends didn't come true every day.

A bell rang. It took a moment for Kelsey to realize it was Will ringing the doorbell and not some bit of magic left over from the enchanted engagement ring. Talk about relief. The door opened.

"It's so good to see you again, Kelsey." Bill Addison greeted her with a hug. With salt-and-pepper hair, he was a more mature version of his son. Same smile, same eyes, same charm. "We're so happy you could help us with Faith's wedding. Starr is excited to see you."

At least someone was happy this morning. Kelsey forced a smile. "Thanks. I'm glad to...help." She stared at father and son and noticed even more similarities between the two, including their names. "Bill and Will? Are you both Williams?"

"I'm William Drake Addison III." Bill motioned to his son. "He's the fourth. I didn't want to upset Starr when all the girls started calling and asking for him so we used different names."

"Dad," Will said in a cautious tone. "I'm sure Kelsey doesn't want to hear this."

"Don't worry, son. I won't start reminiscing about your childhood. Not yet, anyway."

Kelsey chuckled. Will and his father were lucky. She and her brother shared that kind of relationship, but the one between her and her parents was still strained. Years hadn't erased the painful tug-of-war battle they'd put her and her brother through even after the divorce was final.

Will blew out a puff of air. "Just don't pull out the photo albums, okay?"

Bill laughed, deepening the lines on his face. Lines that only added to his attractiveness. Like father, like son. "You'd better get inside before I get in trouble for keeping you out in the cold too long."

Will's forehead wrinkled. "How is Mom feeling this morning?"

"Good. She's feeling very good." Bill's eyes softened to match his voice. "She slept well last night."

"Great." Will's megawatt smile could melt the snow and chase away the most bitter cold. "Let's not keep her waiting."

"She's in the living room."

After hanging up their jackets in the entryway, the two men led Kelsey into the living room. The Stickley furniture—mission-style furnishings—fit perfectly with the craftsman architecture of the house. Wood paneling covered the walls, and beams lined the ceiling. Sunlight flowed in from the windows and illuminated the room. The natural light helped the greener-than-green plants thrive. The windows also provided a stunning view of Lake Tahoe. A crackling fire in the river-rock fireplace warmed the inviting room and completed the picture. Well, almost.

Next to the fireplace sat Starr, looking as lovely as ever. Except for more gray in her brown hair and a simpler hairstyle, she didn't look different except for the wheelchair. Of course, that didn't mean much. Kelsey knew the unseen consequences of a stroke could be the worst.

As soon as Starr saw her, she smiled. Kelsey noticed the slight droop on one side of Starr's mouth and the way her right hand curled as if keeping a treasure hidden from sight.

Will headed directly to his mother and kissed her cheek. "Miss me?"

She caressed his cheek with her left hand. "Always."

Will smiled. "Kelsey agreed to help with the wedding."

"Kelsey." Starr said the name slowly with only a slight slur. "Thank you for coming."

Each word was pronounced carefully, as if it took effort and energy. An enormous amount of relief washed over Kelsey. Thank goodness Starr could talk and make sense. Kelsey remembered her grandmother, who'd found it hard if not impossible to communicate. Aphasia, the doctor had called it. Kelsey pushed the memory aside. It was too late for her grandmother, but Starr... "I hear we have a wedding to put on."

Starr nodded. "Faith has finally found 'the one.'"

Not Starr, too. No doubt the optimism ran in the family. As long as it wasn't contagious... Kelsey pasted on a smile. "Good for Faith."

"But Valentine's isn't too far away." Concern laced Starr's words.

"Don't worry. Everything will be done in time," Kelsey reassured her.

"Knew I c-c-could count on you."

Kelsey grinned at the vote of confidence and caught Will staring at her, a thoughtful smile on his face. Okay, it was better than a frown, but it was a wasted effort. She wasn't about to be intrigued by him, not again. So she ignored him, ignored the way her heart beat in triple time, and focused on Starr instead. "Tell me what you have in mind for the wedding."

Excitement glimmered in Starr's green eyes. She pointed to an alcove off the living room. "My files..."

Bill placed his hand on his wife's shoulder. "Before you girls get wrapped up in wedding talk, we need to eat breakfast, darling."

Love shone in his eyes, and Kelsey realized this couple was one of the lucky ones. One of the few who hadn't abandoned the matrimony ship with the majority of others.

"There's no rush, Mom," Will added. "We have all morning, all day for that matter. Rome wasn't built in a day and neither will Faith's wedding. Remember what the doctor said about overdoing it."

Starr started to say something, then stopped. Even though she nodded as if she agreed, the light faded from her eyes. Kelsey wasn't sure whether Starr was having trouble articulating or if Will's overprotectiveness was getting to her. His love for his mother touched Kelsey's heart, but this wasn't the time for him to be overbearing.

Wanting to put the sparkle back in Starr's eyes, Kelsey kneeled next to her and rested her palm on the smooth metal of the wheelchair. "I want to get started, too," Kelsey whispered, "but trust me, waiting an hour or so won't keep us from planning Faith's wedding."

"Not just any w-w-wedding. This isn't like the other four. We must give her the wedding of her dreams."

Kelsey wasn't sure what the wedding of Faith's dreams entailed. After four completely different weddings, the dream wedding kept changing. And now with the fifth... Kelsey's stomach knotted at the thought. "We can do that."

Touching Kelsey's hand, Starr's eyes reflected her gratitude. "That's why I knew we had to have your help. My family wanted to p-p-postpone the wedding, but it must go on. It's important my baby has someone to look out for her, take care of her. I...Bill and I won't be around forever."

"Don't say that."

"But it's true, and if this wedding isn't perfect..."

Starr sounded so defeated. In the three years Kelsey had known her, Starr had never admitted defeat. Not after Faith's four canceled weddings. Not even after a Starr Properties' Caribbean resort was demolished by a hurricane. Tears pooled in Kelsey's eyes. However subtle, there had been changes due to the stroke. Starr was still determined, but her unwavering self-confidence had disappeared.

"It must be p-p-perfect," Starr insisted.

"I promise you, the wedding will be perfect." And Kelsey knew it would be. No matter what it took, she would not disappoint Starr. Kelsey would give Faith the wedding of her dreams even if it killed her.

It was killing him.

No, Will corrected himself, she was killing him. She, as in Kelsey Armstrong Waters. These past few hours had passed slower than being stuck in a plane at O'Hare waiting for a takeoff slot during a thunderstorm.

Damn Kelsey. Why did she have to be the one making his parents so happy? Starr's recovery and rehabilitation had taken its toll on his parents. Not even Faith or Hope and her kids with their frequent visits over the past few months had managed to make them look so relaxed, so like their old selves, as Kelsey had. Her ability to set people at ease must be useful in her business, but he had to admit with his parents it seemed sincere. Will didn't know whether to be concerned or relieved.

And that made him feel guilty because he saw the changes in his parents. Good changes. Not only had his mother been smiling most of the morning, an improvement over the depression that had plagued her since the stroke, her speech had improved. She still spoke slowly, but talking about the wedding made her pronunciation better with little to no stuttering. Will couldn't believe it. And his father... Over breakfast, he had been completely charmed by Kelsey's witty manner and seemed to shed some of the weight he'd been carrying on his shoulders.

Will should have been happy, but he wasn't. This whole situation was starting to weigh on him. Big time. His mom might be going over ideas with Kelsey, but he would be the one working with her, spending all his time with her, living with her. It would be much easier if she left. Not tomorrow. Not after Faith's wedding. But today.

Starr's laughter reached across the room and warmed Will's heart. It had been too long since his mother had laughed this way. Guilt tightened his throat. How could he be thinking of himself when Kelsey was making such a difference for his parents?

"The theme should revolve around hearts since it's Valentine's Day," Starr proclaimed.

Kelsey jotted in a notebook. "Have the colors been chosen?"

"Faith left it up to me."

The pride in his mother's voice made Will smile. For Mom, he would work with Kelsey. No matter how much her presence unsettled him. He could handle two weeks.

"I was thinking red and pink, but that might be too cliché," Starr said. "Besides, my daughter has never been a big fan of pink. Not even as a little girl. What do you think?"

Kelsey tilted her chin. "It's your choice."

"I just..." Starr sighed. "What would you do if it was your wedding, Kelsey?"

Now this was going to be interesting. Will leaned back on the couch and rested his feet on the coffee table.

Kelsey bit her lip. "My wedding?"

"Yes," his mother said. "What colors would you choose?"

Kelsey hesitated. She crossed her legs and uncrossed them, picked up her notebook then placed it on her lap.

Will grinned. *Way to make her squirm, Mom.*

"What's wrong, dear?" Starr asked.

He nearly laughed at the pained expression on Kelsey's face. Talk about payback for all her anti-marriage talk. And her kiss in the parking lot.

"I'm used to offering ideas, but I don't want my personal likes and dislikes to get in the way of helping you define what the bride and groom—or in this case, you—want. You're the customer."

"Don't worry about that," Starr said. "You've catered to all our whims on the last four weddings. Pretend this time it's yours."

Oh, Mom. You're going to scare her off. Will felt sorry for Kelsey. Well, almost.

"But it's not my...mine," Kelsey explained. "It's Faith's."

Starr smiled. "Humor me."

"Let's see...we had sea-foam green and coral at the first, sage and gold at the second, black and white at the third and cerulean blue and silver at the fourth," Kelsey said.

"Forget about the other weddings. What would *you* do for this one?"

A minute passed. Kelsey's eyes darkened as if she were contemplating the solution to world hunger, not what colors to use in a wedding. "I suppose I'd use intense colors. Red and purple."

"Oh, yes. Faith loves purple." Starr's excitement was almost contagious if one could get excited about colors. "It'll be stunning."

"'Stunning,'" Will echoed though not as enthusiastically as his mother. His comment earned him a glare from Kelsey.

Starr laughed. "Now was that so hard?"

Kelsey smiled, and Will noticed she didn't answer the question. "I'll meet with the florist to discuss the arrangements. Do you have any ideas on flowers?"

Starr nodded. "Please get the folder next to the computer, Will."

His mother's words came slower this time and took effort again. As Will headed toward the desk, he glanced at the grandfather clock on the far wall. They'd been working for almost three hours. "We should call it a day."

"Not yet," Starr said.

Will handed the file to Kelsey and sat in a chair next to his father. The two women seemed to be in a world all their own. Every few minutes he'd catch a word or two. Engraved frames...a string quartet...Canon in D, a DJ, and flowers.

What was it with women and flowers? Red spray

roses, purple violets, grape hyacinths, jasmine, pansies, Laurustinus, synogonium foliage. It was all Greek, or in this case, Latin to him. Enough was enough. Time to call it quits.

"Mom's been going all morning long. Don't you think we should let her relax and take a nap?" he asked Bill.

"She's enjoying herself." His father smiled at the pair of women huddled over a spiral notebook and stacks of file folders and bridal magazines. "Let's not ruin it."

"But the doctor said—"

"A smile on your mother's face is the best medicine," Bill said. "Trust me."

Will wasn't so sure. Sure she looked happy, but what about the dark circles under her eyes? Being that tired couldn't be good for her. As he watched her, his jaw tensed. His mother was still beautiful, but she'd lost that spark in her eyes, the vitality that used to radiate from her. She'd faded from a vibrant color into a pastel. His chest tightened.

"That should do it for now." Kelsey closed her notebook. "We've got enough to get started with."

"If you have any questions, give me a call." Starr patted Kelsey's hand. "And don't forget to keep in mind what I said about the other…thing."

Kelsey grinned. "I won't."

The edges of his mother's mouth turned up slightly. Even tired, she still managed a smile. "It'll save us so much time when we plan the next wedding."

"Next wedding?" Will stared at his mother, then at Kelsey, who merely shrugged. "What are you talking about? Faith won't be getting married again."

"She won't." Mischief glimmered in Starr's tired eyes. "But you will."

What had he done to deserve this? He'd been a dutiful son, a loyal brother, a faithful husband and a loving uncle. But he wasn't going to get married again. No way. No how.

Not even for his mother.

Will leaned against the counter in his parents' kitchen feeling as though he'd been shanghaied. His father was giving Kelsey a tour of the house while his mother sat across from Will with a white envelope on her lap and a strange smile on her face. Maybe this was all a big joke to her. Then again...

"What's this all about, Mom?"

"I hope your father doesn't take Kelsey into the exercise room. It's a mess from my physical therapy."

"Kelsey won't mind."

Starr eyes gleamed with interest. "She's very attractive."

Will wasn't about to go there. He groaned. "I'm not getting married again so whatever you've got up your sleeve—"

"I want you to read this." She handed him the envelope. "After the stroke, I had one of my nurses help me write everything down in case I didn't have the chance to tell you myself. I've been waiting for the right time, but I don't know if there is a right time."

The emotion in her voice concerned Will. He'd never seen his mother like this, not even in the hospital. A quick, disturbing thought raced through him, but he pushed it aside. His mother couldn't predict when she was going to have another stroke. Still, apprehension remained. He ran his fingertip along the seal of the envelope, but didn't open it.

Starr took a breath and exhaled slowly. "Please read it."

With a sinking feeling in his stomach, he ripped open the envelope and unfolded the letter.

My dearest son,
I'm writing this from my heart. I hope you will take it that way and not be upset at me. First let me say, I love your father. I truly believe he is my "one." He's not only my right and left hand, he's my heart. But after my stroke, I realized it wouldn't be fair to him to live the rest of his life alone if I died. I'd want him to have a second chance at love.

His hand trembled. "You can't be serious."
Starr's tired eyes pleaded with him. "Keep reading."

Anything else would be a disservice to the love we've shared all these years, to the values we lived by and instilled in you and your sisters.
I believe Sara would feel the same way. I loved her as if she was my own daughter, but you both were so young when you married. You were traveling, and she was away at school. And though you loved each other deeply, the times you spent together were nothing more than extended honeymoons. Fate stepped in before you could have anything more.

Jagged raw feelings sliced through his heart. He crinkled the edge of the letter. "You're wrong, Mom. Sara and I...we had so much together. Our marriage was perfect."

"But Sara's gone." Starr reached out to touch his arm. "Please read the entire letter."

Will didn't want to read any more. He wanted to shred the letter into tiny pieces and toss it in the garbage can. He continued reading instead.

It's time for you to put the past behind you. You shouldn't grow old alone, loving a memory, when you can grow old with a loving woman by your side. It's time, Will. You need to find a woman to love and marry. You deserve a second chance at love. It's what Sara would want.

He felt as if he'd been sucker punched. His mother didn't know what she was saying. She couldn't believe what she'd written. Not after all the things she'd told him growing up. All those stories about true love and happily-ever-after she'd told him and his sister. The stories about the Addisons who had come before them and how they had a tradition to follow, to uphold. "Does Dad know you wrote this?"

She gazed at him through lowered lashes. "No, when it's time..."

"Mom—"

"I love you so much and I want you to be happy."

"You have no idea what would make me happy." Will's tone was harsher than he'd intended, but he couldn't help himself. This was his worst nightmare come true.

Starr smiled. "Thank you."

"For what? I yelled at you." He brushed his hand through his hair. "I'm sorry, Mom."

"Don't be sorry." Her eyes twinkled. "You didn't yell, you finally talked to me like a real person, not a fragile piece of crystal about to fall off the shelf."

"Is that what this is about?"

"No," she admitted. "It's about you moving on. You don't have to do it today or tomorrow, but I want you to think about what I wrote."

Will didn't need to think about it. There was nothing left for him to do. He had moved on. Moving on did not include remarrying. He folded the letter and jammed the paper into his jacket pocket. His mother was wrong, but this must have been a hard letter for her to compose. "I appreciate your concern, Mom. Every thing you do reminds me how lucky I am to have a mother who loves her kids as much as you love us."

Chapter Five

As Will paced the length of his living room and back, Kelsey thumbed through the preference sheets Faith had filled out over the years. Four different sets. Four different weddings to four different grooms. A deck of cards would be easier to make sense of and sort through. Perhaps with a little help... Kelsey glanced up at Will. "It isn't so bad."

He tightened his mouth to a thin, grim line. "Easy for you to say."

He was acting as if someone had stolen a closetfull of Manolo Blahnik shoes. Not that Kelsey hadn't felt the same way when she realized what the next fourteen days held for her and that she was going to need every bit of help Will was offering. But first she had to help him get through this thing with his mother. Kelsey wasn't sure what had happened while she'd been with his father, but Will had been stoic and silent since they'd returned to his house. It had to end. She couldn't afford any distractions with all the work they had to do. "Starr loves you."

He stopped dead in his tracks. "She wants me to get married again."

He said the word "married" as if it were the name of a virus with a one-hundred-percent fatality rate. Not that Kelsey didn't feel the same way. "Starr only wants you to be happy."

"I am happy."

About as happy as a four-year-old asked to wear a tuxedo and be the ring bearer at a wedding and endure the torturous ordeal of standing still. Kelsey smiled.

Will frowned. "This isn't funny."

"Oh, it's very funny. If you could see your face." The only things missing were crocodile tears running down his cheeks and a pout on those kissable lips. Will was all man, but if he ever had a son, Kelsey knew what he would look like. Cute wouldn't even begin to describe him. She felt a little hitch in her heart. "You don't look very happy right now."

"Imagine how you would look if your mother wanted to marry you off A.S.A.P."

"Not pretty." Just the thought horrified Kelsey, but marriage was the last thing her mother would ever suggest to her. Besides, Mom was too involved in her own life and marital status to care about Kelsey's.

"Exactly."

"But Starr's not trying to marry you off. At least not until after Faith's wedding."

"Still not funny."

"Come on," Kelsey urged in her most encouraging you-haven't-gotten-fat-since-ordering-the-wedding-dress voice. "She's only looking out for your best interest."

He stared at her as if she'd grown horns and turned green. "My best interest?"

Kelsey nodded. "She wants to see her children—all of her children—settled."

"Settled does not equal married."

"Maybe not to you. Or me," she admitted. "But it does to Starr. She doesn't want you to be alone."

"I'm not alone," he countered. "I have Midas. I..." He frowned. "Why am I even discussing this? I'm not getting married. I couldn't marry again. My marriage was perfect."

Perfect. Just the idea made Kelsey squirm in her seat.

"Sara was my life," Will continued. "How do you replace all that?"

You don't. But Kelsey knew better than to answer out loud. Neither of them wanted to marry, but for completely different reasons. "Try to see it from your mother's point of view. She's trying to get all her ducks in a row, so to speak, in case something happens—"

"Nothing is going to happen to her." The determined set of his chin told Kelsey that wasn't an option, not on Will's watch. If only life were that simple and predictable.

"She's tying up loose ends because she's feeling vulnerable right now." And Kelsey could see Starr wasn't the only one feeling that way. Kelsey's heart went out not only to Starr, but to Will, too. "She only wants the best for you and your sisters."

"What's 'best' can't be defined by our marital status. If you read her letter..."

"What letter?"

A vein on his neck throbbed. "It...it's not important."

Kelsey wasn't quite sure she believed him, but that

wasn't her concern right now. "Listen, your mother's simply getting carried away with Faith's wedding. Once it's over, your marital status won't be an issue. I've seen it happen lots of times."

"I don't think so."

"Time will tell," Kelsey said. "But right now I need you to put it on the back burner and focus on helping me with Faith's wedding."

He cocked a brow. "You want my help?"

Kelsey hesitated. Asking for help wasn't easy for her to do, but in this case it was a necessity. "Yes."

He raised a brow. "Why the sudden change?"

She shrugged. "It's not really a change, per se, but certain things aren't as finalized as I'd hoped."

"My mother said she had everything planned."

"She did," Kelsey said in her most tactful voice. "She has everything planned conceptually. Making it happen is something else."

"How much do we need to do?"

Kelsey took a calming breath. "Pretty much everything except the invitations."

Will combed his hand through his hair. Man, she loved his hair. Kelsey gritted her teeth. No, she didn't.

"Where do we start?" he asked.

"I need to see Faith's dress. Starr said it's here."

"No one can see it. Faith's order."

"Fine." Kelsey pursed her lips. "But you can be the one to explain to her why her bridal bouquet clashes with her gown."

"Flowers can't clash with a gown."

Men. Kelsey rolled her eyes. Gorgeous or not, they didn't get it. "Oh, yes, they can."

"How?"

"Where would you like me to start? How about with

the different styles and fabrics used in wedding dresses and how that can be overwhelmed by the flowers or vice versa? Or would you rather hear about the various shapes of bouquets and flowers you can use that can make or break a gown? Teardrop, heart, nosegay. Would you like me to go on?''

The dazed look on his face was priceless. He might have been comfortable in her overtly feminine office and not have too much of a problem helping with wedding plans, but details of gowns and flowers were out of his realm. Totally. Kelsey chuckled.

"You can look," he said finally. "The dress is hanging in her room."

Kelsey followed him up the stairs. Cute butt. She'd love to see him in a pair of Levi's jeans. No, she balled her fists, she wouldn't.

"Did my mom tell you she wanted Faith to wear her wedding dress this time, but Faith said no?"

"She didn't." Poor Starr. Many mothers-of-the-brides wanted to pass on their gowns to their daughters. Kelsey's own mother had a personal collection of wedding gowns, dresses and suits in every style from traditional to sleek sophistication, but luckily Kelsey would never be in need of one. "Perhaps a granddaughter will want to wear Starr's gown someday."

"That would make my mom happy."

Kelsey smiled. "Or perhaps your bride—"

"Don't say it, don't even think it." Will grimaced. "You don't understand. If my mother got wind of that…"

"She'd have her dress cleaned, pressed and ready to go."

Will nodded. "She'd want you to find the perfect veil to match."

"Shoes, too."

He smiled. "And a coordinating bouquet. You wouldn't want the flowers to overwhelm the gown," he imitated her.

With a laugh, she smacked his arm. Will opened the door to Faith's room. Kelsey stepped in and nearly fell over.

She glanced around in surprise—no, shock. Romantic, soft and fluffy described the room and the furnishings. Three adjectives Kelsey would never have used to describe the fifth-time bride-to-be. Three adjectives that perfectly described Kelsey's room at her father's house. "This is Faith's room?"

Will nodded. "You're pale. Is something wrong?"

Wrong, everything was wrong. This had to be an anomaly. Kelsey thought she and Faith had nothing in common except their gender. Kelsey was totally different than the fickle starlet. Faith had four ex-fiancés and a current one; Kelsey had never been nor planned on being engaged. Faith was adored by millions; Kelsey preferred to remain in the background. Yet you'd never know there was a difference walking in here.

"This...this could be *my* room. My room when I was growing up."

"I don't picture you in a room like this."

"I didn't picture *Faith* in a room like this." Kelsey ran her fingers over the wedding-ring-patterned quilt covering the queen-size oak four-poster. Okay, her own bed was cherry, but close enough. Too close. Had Faith's grandmother quilted her bedcover as Kelsey's had? "But the similarities...it's kind of eerie."

His brows furrowed. "Your bedroom was really like this?"

She nodded. "My bedroom at my father's house.

When he finally convinced a judge to give him visitation rights, he set up rooms for us." She picked up one of the teddy bears sitting on top of the quilt in front of a pile of lacy pillows of various shapes and sizes. "We got to help decorate the rooms when we went to live with him after my mother married husband number two. Otto was allergic to children. Or so he claimed. My brother had to share a room with Samuel, one of our ex-stepbrothers, and later with Jimmy, another one of them, but I had my own room. Cade and I would spend hours in my room. It was our..."

"Your what?"

"Our safe place," Kelsey admitted, remembering how walking into her room had made her feel. Safe and secure and whole. "The room has always been the one constant in our life. Mom was always moving into whatever new house came with her new husband, but Dad tried to keep whatever he could the same. The room hasn't changed except I have a new stepsister living there now."

"I can't imagine," Will said.

"Don't even try." Kelsey walked to the vanity table and traced one of the hand-painted roses with her fingertip. "I had one of these. And a chaise like Faith's." As childhood memories washed over Kelsey, she smiled. "Cade and I used them to play shrink."

"Shrink?"

"One of us would be the psychiatrist and sit at the vanity. The other would lie on the chaise and tell the shrink what was bothering us. It was easier talking to each other than all the professionals our parents kept taking us to so we'd stay well adjusted."

"Kelsey, this marriage aversion really runs deep for you, doesn't it?"

Before she could answer, Will touched her shoulder. The small gesture of comfort meant more than it should, and she ignored the impulse to move closer to him. Safe and strong and perfect. All the things Will was; all things he could never be for her. A dull ache spread through her, and she shrugged away from his hand.

"It's okay." Kelsey forced a smile. "Lots of people grow up in dysfunctional families. Present company excluded."

Will smiled. "I never knew functional was the minority."

"You'd be surprised. But I must admit, I envy your childhood, growing up with parents who loved and respected each other must have been nice."

"Don't forget, childhood is only a small part of our lives. It's who we are now that counts."

"So true." She glanced around the room one last time. Time to be who *she* was. "Where's the dress?"

"Hanging in the closet." Will motioned to the double closet doors. "I'm going to wait in the hall. Let me know when you're done."

"You don't want to take a peek?"

"And suffer the wrath of Faith? No thanks." He walked to the doorway. "You might want to prepare yourself."

"Prepare myself?"

"My mother said this gown was different."

How different could different be? Each of Faith's four wedding dresses were different. A beaded mermaid gown for the Under the Sea wedding extravaganza; an empire-waist period gown for the Jane Austin Regency wedding ball; a Vera Wang original for the New Year's Eve millennium bash, and a silk sarong for the barefoot-on-the-beach soiree. Funny how all her weddings seemed to correspond with whatever movie Faith was making at the time. Speaking of which...

"What is Faith filming right now?"

"It's a high-tech, high-budget alien-from-outer-space movie. She's saves the universe from destruction and falls in love during the process." Will stepped into the doorway and turned his back to her so he faced the hallway. "Go ahead and look."

Kelsey wasn't sure she wanted to. Aliens and a Valentine's wedding? Laser guns and hearts. Picturing a silver lamé wedding gown, she sighed. That wouldn't quite go with the wedding she and Starr had discussed. Oh, well...

Kelsey took a deep breath and opened the closet door. The dress was covered with a piece of muslin. Hello, sci-fi bride. She pulled the muslin away and gasped.

"Is it that bad?" Will called.

"Yes. I mean, no. Not bad. Not at all. Different, yes, but..." Kelsey struggled for the right words to say. "It's breathtaking."

Her pulse raced, and her heart felt as if it had lodged in her throat. Forget about high-tech and aliens. Faith had stepped back in time when selecting this gown. Edwardian. That was the time period. And Kelsey couldn't believe it. The vintage-style lace gown looked as if it had been made for the veil and wreath she'd been trying on when Will walked in her office.

Talk about a perfect match. What was the word for it—synchronicity. She should have been disappointed Faith would be wearing the ensemble, but Kelsey wasn't. Not when all three pieces looked as if they were made for one another. Destiny? Kelsey wondered. Even a realist such as her couldn't ignore Fate. Not when it was right under your nose and making you take notice.

Kelsey fought the urge to touch the lace. She didn't want to snag the delicate fabric or smudge it with oil from her fingertips.

What she really wanted to do was to try the dress on for herself. Talk about a first. Even with all the gowns she'd seen over the years, not one had ever appealed to her the way this one did. This gown was practically calling her name, begging her to put it on to see how it looked.

The scent of roses filled the air. Kelsey glanced around the room. More stuffed animals, a few pictures in pewter frames. But no flowers or potpourri she could see. Must be a sachet in the closet somewhere. Kelsey had sachets all over her room. No doubt with all the other similarities, Faith had the same.

Will cleared his throat. "Have you seen enough?"

No. Kelsey blinked. She could never get enough of this dress. Lace covered the entire gown except for a small amount of netting at the neckline. The long sleeves tapered to a slight point. Intricate flowers had been woven into the lace. Flowers she thought would match those on the wreath. And the flowers for the bouquet...

Kelsey clasped her hands together. She knew exactly what type of bouquet and flowers would go perfectly.

With a sigh, she dropped the muslin over the dress and closed the closet door. Turning, Kelsey stared at Will's backside. "I've seen enough."

For now, she thought to herself and smiled.

February 2

It was too early to get up. Not even Midas was about to stir at this hour. Will hit the snooze button on his alarm and yawned. He needed more sleep. No, he actually needed to go to sleep. Too bad his mind wouldn't turn off. He wanted to blame his restlessness on his mother's letter, but that had only kept him up half the night. The other half was Kelsey's fault.

Thoughts of her were messing with his head. A physical attraction was one thing, but he was drawn to much more than her hair and her smile and her kiss. Last night had only been the beginning. He wanted to spend more time with her, to learn more about her and to peel away the layers until he could see exactly who she was.

Too bad she was his sister's wedding consultant. And, if his mother had his way, she'd be his, too.

The alarm sounded again. This time Will got up. He'd promised to take Kelsey to the inn bright and early this morning. It was early, but forget about bright. Not even the sun was up.

Thirty minutes later they were off. Using a flashlight to light the way, he led Kelsey down the path to the inn. Driving would have been warmer, but it wouldn't have been as fast or as secluded. No matter what, they couldn't let the press see Kelsey. And he could use the walk to clear his head.

Their boots crunched on the layer of new snow. The sound filled the silence of the frosty dawn. Not even a bird was up at this hour.

"We're almost there." Will glanced back and aimed his flashlight at Kelsey. He almost didn't recognize her. A wool cap covered her hair. Gloves kept her fingers warm. Her cheeks and nose looked pink. She looked young and vulnerable. Protectiveness crept in, but the last person he felt like was her older brother. "Cold?" he asked.

"A little." She shoved one of her hands into her pocket. "But I'll survive."

Survive. That's what he'd been doing each and every day since Sara died. Suddenly it didn't seem like enough.

His gaze met hers. Will stood transfixed, watching each cloud of breath rise from Kelsey's mouth, from her lips. He remembered how those lips felt against his. Warm and soft and seductive. Lips made for kissing. Kissing him.

Forget about the freezing temperature outside. He was feeling so warm at the moment, he might as well have been in the tropics not Tahoe. He didn't need his jacket. Or his hat. Or his gloves. He continued to stare.

She glanced down at the snow, breaking the invisible bond between them. The silence lengthened between them.

Will needed more sleep to clear the fog in his brain. He hadn't wanted to think about her kiss again. Not when he couldn't stop thinking about her. She was messing up his nice orderly world. Where were his memories of Sara and her kisses? He was going to have to keep his distance from Kelsey. Maybe it would be better if she stayed somewhere else.

"You said the inn isn't much farther," she said finally.

"It's not." He started back up the path. "We're almost there."

When they reached the inn, Will concentrated on getting to the service entrance without being seen. Once inside, the heat warmed them. As did the cups of coffee he snagged from the kitchen. He led Kelsey through a pair of double doors and flicked on the lights. The wood parquet floors gleamed. Crisp, white linen tablecloths covered the tables. Each chair was perfectly aligned in front of an elaborately folded linen napkin. Another fine

job by the Starr Properties' staff. Will smiled. "What
do you think?"

"The room is lovely." She stared up at one of the
four iron chandeliers hanging from the beamed ceiling.
Kelsey's chestnut braid fell back. The tilt of her head
emphasized the curve of her neck. A neck that seemed
to be asking for nibbles and kisses. But not from him.
Definitely not from him. She touched one of the chair
backs. "Have you made alternate dining arrangements
for your hotel guests on the day of the event?"

Event, not wedding. She was good, very good. "We
have."

She studied every inch of the room, including the
wood molding and the pictures gracing the wall. She
measured every inch, too.

Will tried not to notice how her well-worn, well-
fitting jeans cupped her bottom so nicely. He failed. Not
a big deal, he rationalized. No crime in looking.

She stood in front of the walk-in-size fireplace.
"Wow, what a huge fireplace. It's beautiful."

Will smiled. "When we were younger, Faith saw
these life-size stockings and asked if we could buy them
and hang them here for Santa."

"What did your parents say?"

"Yes. Faith was a real cutie and usually got what she
wanted. Good thing in this instance. We still have those
same stockings, and Santa fills them every year."

"We had so many different stockings I think Santa
sometimes got confused." With a faraway look in her
eyes, she stared into the fireplace. "Before we left Chicago and moved to Beverly Hills, Cade and I would
spend Christmas Eve with one of my parents and Christmas day with the other. My parents always tried to
outdo the other with presents. One year there were so

many presents we couldn't even step into my mother's living room. It was obscene. My dad's house was almost as bad.''

"Every kid dreams of a Christmas like that.''

Kelsey nodded. "You know what my favorite gift was that year?''

"A stuffed animal or piece of jewelry?''

"A framed picture of my family. My mom, Dad, Cade and me.'' Kelsey's smile reached all the way to her eyes. "My grandmother had my mother pick a picture so she could have it framed, and my mom actually gave her one of the four of us taken before the divorce.''

Will not only heard but saw on her face how much one photograph of her family had meant to Kelsey. He tried to imagine what her life was like as a child, pushed and pulled between two parents who didn't love each other. Not only at Christmastime, but every day of her life. He couldn't. "Kelsey—''

"This is the perfect setting for the reception, but the ceremony—'' she clicked the top of her pen "—we shouldn't have the ceremony here.''

Back to business. Just when it was getting interesting again. He wished he knew where her On/Off switch was located. Still, he respected how hard she worked. "Why?''

"If we hold the ceremony elsewhere and Faith cancels, none of the party guests will know a wedding was in the works. They'll think they were only invited to your parents' anniversary celebration. No decorations to remove. No sitting to rearrange. No explanations necessary.''

"None will be needed,'' Will said with confidence. "Faith isn't going to cancel.''

"You sound so certain.''

"If you could see her and Trent together... It's the real thing."

"What about Faith's four other weddings and fiancés?"

"What do you mean?"

"You and your parents are die-hard romantics. What happened to Faith?"

"Nothing happened to her. She got engaged to the wrong men, but now that she's found Trent, everything will work out fine."

The intense look in Kelsey's eyes cut through him, made him feel naked and on view. He didn't like the feeling. "You honestly believe that?" she asked.

"Heart and soul."

She hesitated, her eyes full of questions. "I'd still like to have a backup plan in case Trent turns out not to be 'the one.' We can have the minister renew your parents' vows if the wedding gets canceled. The renewal can take place here and we'll clean up the wedding ceremony site later."

"Where do you want to hold the ceremony?"

"At your house. What do you think?"

He remembered how she described the wedding decorations when she'd first walked into his house. "My mother told you to do what you want. To act as if it's your wedding. Would you like to get married at my house?"

"It's Faith's wedding, and I believe she would like it." Kelsey spoke the words in that cool businesslike manner of hers, but not before he saw the slight quiver of her lower lip.

Not so cool and collected, after all. Another layer to figure out. Will smiled. "Would you like it?"

"This isn't about me."

But it was. He could tell by her voice and her eyes. That hard shell of hers was showing signs of cracking and Will wanted to be the one to rip it apart. "Would you like it?" he repeated.

"Yes, but it's your house."

Watching the anticipation mount in Kelsey's expressive eyes as she waited for his answer made Will want to take forever to reply. Knowing he was treading into dangerous waters, he looked away. "We can hold the ceremony at my house."

She rewarded him with a wide grin. A kiss would have been better. But kissing Kelsey was a no-no as his sister Hope would say to his niece and nephews. A big no-no. As was thinking about her lips, her neck, and anything else. No touching, either. He brushed his hand through his hair.

"Thanks," Kelsey said. "I thank you, and I'm sure Faith will thank you, too."

Chapter Six

It was nearly midnight. The comfortable bed upstairs had Kelsey's name written all over it, but sleep could wait a few hours. The more she got done tonight, the better handle she would have on the wedding. Besides, ever since she'd snuck into Faith's room two hours ago and stolen another look at her gown, Kelsey had been inspired. Okay, she stifled a yawn, she was a little tired, but inspired nonetheless. She placed her water glass in the kitchen sink.

Will entered and stretched his arms over his head. "This wedding planning reminds me of cramming for finals."

She smiled. "It's not that bad."

"No, but we deserve a break." He motioned to the coffeemaker on the counter. "Coffee?"

"Sounds good to me." She tucked a stray strand of hair back into her braid. "We might need the caffeine to stay awake."

"Don't tell me we're going to be pulling an all-nighter."

"Okay, I won't tell you."

He groaned. "I'm having a finals week flashback." As she removed the pot, he plugged in the coffeemaker. "At least it's a pleasant memory of opening one of my care packages."

"Care packages?"

He placed a filter inside the coffeemaker. "My mom always sent care packages during finals week. She filled them with of all sorts of goodies to keep me going as I studied and crammed. I can still taste the homemade chocolate-chip cookies."

A familiar ache and longing squeezed Kelsey's heart. She turned on the faucet and water streamed out. "The only thing my parents ever sent were checks to cover tuition and my living expenses."

"At least they paid for your college."

She filled the pot and poured it into the coffeemaker. "Didn't your parents?"

"Yes, but not everyone is as lucky."

Will was more than lucky. He'd been blessed to be born into a family like the Addisons. Not a messed-up family like hers. "You can say that again."

He measured out the dark grounds and dumped them inside the filter. "What do you mean?

"Your family is 'Leave it to Beaver' or 'Father Knows Best' come to life. I wish they could adopt me." Guilt raced through her. Her family might not be perfect, but they loved her. Still the Addisons held such an appeal to her. Kelsey replaced the pot.

As Will turned on the coffeemaker, he laughed, a rich sound that was as smooth as warm caramel sauce. "Sorry, two sisters are more than enough. Now your brother would be a different story. I always wanted a younger brother.''

Now that was funny. Kelsey chuckled. "Cade doesn't even like to claim any relation to the Armstrongs. He would never cut it as an Addison. Your family is so normal, he'd say you're abnormal."

"We're not that different from other families," Will said.

She rolled her eyes. "Your family is perfect."

"No one is perfect, especially my family."

"Your parents are still together."

"True, but they've had their ups and downs."

"I don't believe it." As she grabbed the sugar holder, the scent of freshly brewing coffee filled the air. "What about the Addisons claim to one love in a lifetime?"

"Even true love hits a bump every now and then." Will removed two mugs from the cupboard and placed them on the counter. "My parents didn't always get along. I remember this one time I was asleep, but their yelling woke me up. My sisters, too. We stood at the top of the stairs listening to the screaming and the shouting. I still remember the tears streaming down Faith's cheeks. She stood between Hope and me, holding on to our hands."

Similar memories washed over Kelsey. The fear of watching her world fall apart, of having everything she'd come to count on torn away. Her stomach knotted and bile rose in her throat. "You just described a scene from my house. Cade and I would wake up to the yelling and the screaming. We'd sit together in his closet until we heard the doors slam, and it would be over. For a little while at least."

"The doors never slammed at our house. But that didn't make it any better. Especially this time. My mom broke down crying. I'd never heard her sob like that. She was so exhausted, raising me and my sisters, running the Starr B and B and helping to renovate the inn. But my father couldn't understand why she couldn't give him the attention he wanted. Mom said she didn't have any energy left for him by the end of the day. My father said she just didn't love him anymore."

Kelsey knew how much that must have hurt Will and his sisters to hear. Her parents once claimed they'd never loved each other to begin with. Pain gripped her heart, and she slouched against the counter. "What happened?"

"Faith ran down the stairs begging them not to get a divorce. She always had a flair for the dramatic, even when she was little." Will poured the steaming coffee into the mugs and handed Kelsey one. "My parents were mortified when they realized we were there and had witnessed everything. They had the three of us sit with them in the living room for a long talk about what we'd heard. They apologized and told us not to worry about a divorce and explained how they would work through their problems."

Kelsey had heard that over and over again. Until it had become white noise to her and Cade. She added a teaspoon of sugar to her coffee and stirred. "Easier said than done."

"They did exactly what they said they would do."

She held the spoon in midair. "How?"

"They made a weekly date night and would never cancel unless blood, a fever, or a trip to the hospital was involved." Coffee in hand, Will leaned against the counter. "My dad took over some of the B and B work, hired a project manager for the inn remodeling and brought home a pizza every Friday night so my mom didn't have to cook."

"That's...amazing. It's hard to believe they worked it out." A stab of envy pierced her heart. "If that were my parents, my father would have gone out and found the attention he wanted elsewhere. Who am I kidding?" Kelsey stared into her coffee. "That's what he did. My mother, too. I just wish..."

"What?"

"That my parents could have been more like your parents and thought about how their actions affected us." Her hand trembled as she held on to her mug. "They didn't even come and tell us they were getting a divorce. My mom said to pack a bag because we were going on a trip. She stashed us away with a distant Armstrong cousin so my father couldn't find us. She didn't even let us say goodbye to him. My dad was frantic, and my mother loved every minute of it. Things went downhill from there." Kelsey gripped her mug with both hands so she wouldn't drop it. "My parents couldn't work through anything, not even when it came to me and my brother."

"We aren't destined to follow in our parents' footsteps."

"I suppose not, but we can learn from their mistakes." The heat from the mug warmed her hands, took away the chill that had taken hold of her. "I've over-analyzed what happened to my parents and their subsequent spouses. There's no chance of ever getting it right. I'm certain of that."

"Sure, with that attitude. But, Kelsey, you can get it right." The sincerity in his eyes tugged at her heart. Such a romantic. "When I married Sara, I didn't expect to have smooth sailing, but I knew no matter what came up we'd make it. We'd have a couple of kids, a cat and a dog." Will shrugged. "I got the cat."

"You got more than that."

His faint smile held a touch of sadness. "I know."

"You could try again. Go on a few dates," Kelsey suggested.

"I date," he said quickly. "I'm only human."

"Thanks for clarifying that point."

He chuckled. "Dating is okay, but in the end it never goes anywhere. What Sara and I had...you don't find that every day."

"I'm sure you don't." Kelsey took a sip of her coffee. "You must miss her."

His smile disappeared and he placed his empty cup on the counter. "I do."

Kelsey couldn't imagine what he'd gone through. From falling in love to losing the love of his life, all those feelings, emotions, were so foreign to her.

She refilled his mug. "So are you ready to pull an all-nighter?"

February 3

So much for pulling an all-nighter.

The crick in Will's neck was about to kill him, but that's what he got for falling asleep on the couch. He stretched only to find his legs tangled in something warm and soft and... His eyes sprang open.

Kelsey.

She was sound asleep on the opposite end of the couch. Her legs entwined with his across the large sofa. Her lips curved upward, and Will wondered what dream had put the peaceful smile on her face. Her dark lashes shadowed her fair skin. The mole on her cheek seemed to wink at him as if it wanted a kiss.

Right here, right now, all her barriers were down, and he liked that. She wasn't the hardworking wedding consultant. She wasn't the cynical realist who didn't believe in happily-ever-afters. She was Sleeping Beauty. All she needed was a kiss to wake her up...

His chest tightened.

He was no Prince Charming. Not even close. Prince Charming wouldn't be watching her sleep like this. He wouldn't be feeling like such a trespasser.

But something about her drove his curiosity. Nothing about Kelsey was surface level, and there was more to her cynicism than met the eye. Thanks to their conversation last night, he had a better understanding of why Kelsey felt the way she did about love and marriage. He couldn't blame her after everything she and her brother had been through. But Will blamed her parents.

A sigh escaped Kelsey's lips. She shifted, rubbing her calf against his. A rush of heat raced through him. He allowed himself a minute to enjoy the moment. Lying together this way with Kelsey felt so good, so natural.

His muscles tensed. There was nothing natural about it. Strange. That's what it was.

Will had been surrounded by women his entire life. His mother, his sisters, his wife. But Kelsey didn't fit into any of the usual categories. She wasn't even a lover. Yet he was feeling things he hadn't felt since Sara...

Will untangled his legs and sat up straight. How could the feelings be the same? Kelsey was nothing like Sara. Tall and brunette, Kelsey was the antithesis of his petite, blond wife.

But the differences went deeper than the physical.

Gentle, soft-spoken Sara would have been bowled over by tell-it-like-it-is Kelsey. His wife had been easygoing without Kelsey's drive and determination. Sara was the perfect wife; Kelsey didn't believe in marriage. One was milk and apple pie, the other champagne and crème brûlée.

Yet both women made him smile, made him laugh, made him feel a certain something he couldn't quite name. A feeling that wasn't going away even after he'd thought about it for a minute or two.

Kelsey blinked open her eyes. "Wh-what happened?"

"Resting our eyes turned into a rest-of-the-night snooze session."

As she sat upright, worry creased her forehead. "We slept here? Together?"

She sounded like a puritan. Will bit back a chuckle. "If you're worried about your virtue, don't be. We had a chaperon."

Midas slept on the back of the couch. Kelsey looked at him. "What's that noise he's making?"

"That's how he breathes."

"Are you sure?"

"Positive." A memory of a similar conversation brought a smile to Will's face. Maybe Kelsey and Sara had something in common—a concern for Midas.

"You noisy kitty you." Kelsey kissed Midas's head. "You just have to do everything your own way, including breathe. But that's okay, handsome."

As she nuzzled her cheek against Midas's fur, a tender warmth wrapped around Will like a blanket. Kelsey glanced over and saw him staring at her, but she didn't look away. Two lines formed above her nose, and she straightened. "We have an appointment at the bakery. We don't want to be late, and I need a shower."

In the space of a second, Sleeping Beauty had been replaced by the Ultimate Wedding Planner. Will shouldn't have been disappointed, but for some strange reason he was. He liked the softer, more playful Kelsey.

Half an hour later, she met him downstairs again. She'd tucked her hair into a wool cap and was wearing a pair of black slacks and a red sweater. She'd put on a pair of round sunglasses and shrugged on a long, over-size black coat he'd borrowed from Hope's closet. "Do you think anyone will recognize me?"

He barely recognized her, especially in the baggy coat. If he remembered correctly, Hope had worn that when she was pregnant with his nephew, Connor. He wondered if Kelsey ever thought about having kids. "You're safe."

She smiled. "Are you ready to go?"

No complaints, no yawns. Nothing. Not even a word about sleeping on the couch with him.

No big deal, he figured.

Yeah, right, an inner voice mocked.

Will ignored it. Ignored the strange feelings clamoring for attention inside him. Ignored how all of this had to do with Kelsey, not Sara.

Kelsey stood outside the bakery with Will. Her disguise seemed to be working. No one seemed to be paying any attention to them. She probably could have come up with something more clever than a big coat, hat and sunglasses, but there hadn't been time. She needed to order a wedding cake and to do that she needed to taste cake samples.

From the street, Fitzpatrick's Baked Goods looked like a quaint bakery, a mom-and-pop shop you might find on any main street, in any small town in America.

According to Will, the Fitzpatrick family supplied baked goods to local restaurants, ski resorts and hotels, including Starr Lake Inn.

The bakery was also gaining a reputation for its cakes—birthday, wedding, you name it. The Fitzpatrick's oldest daughter, Molly, baked cakes that Will described as sinful. This, Kelsey had to taste. Not only the cake, but what Will considered sinful. That in itself warranted a visit to the bakery.

Will opened the glass door for her and a bell jangled. Kelsey entered the bakery. The smell of vanilla, chocolate and a hint of cinnamon lingered in the air, greeting her like an old friend. Glass display cases held a variety of cakes, pastries, tortes, breads and cookies. Round tables covered with blue-and-white checked tablecloths and white wood tole-painted chairs filled the bakery and were crowded with customers dressed in every type of ski attire imaginable. The din of the crowd rose above the morning's ski report being broadcast over speakers placed in the ceiling.

A woman in her early twenties with a fair complexion and copper-colored hair greeted Will with a hug and kiss. Kelsey's stomach flip-flopped at the sight.

Will kept his arm around the woman's shoulders. "Kelsey Armstrong Waters meet Molly Fitzpatrick."

The woman was the cake-maker he'd talked about. Kelsey didn't understand why that made the knot in her stomach loosen. She extended her hand. "Nice to meet you."

As Molly shook her hand, she smiled, a friendly smile full of warmth and enthusiasm. Freckles dotted the bridge of her nose and cheeks. "The pleasure is mine, Ms. Waters."

"Kelsey."

A dimple appeared on Molly's left cheek. "Kelsey, it is. Follow me."

Molly led them to a room in the back. "Will said you were trying to keep a low profile, so I thought you might want to taste the samples in private."

"Thank you." Inside the room, Kelsey removed her sunglasses. Not only were small plates with cake samples set out next to a pitcher of water and cups, but actual cakes of varying sizes and shapes covered the other tables. Cakes that made Kelsey's mouth water. If they tasted as good as they looked... "I've heard glowing reports about your cakes."

"And I've heard the same about your weddings, though Will tells me this one is an anniversary party for his parents."

"Yes, they'll be renewing their vows and the party will be a wedding reception for them."

Molly's green-eyed gaze met Will's. "How romantic for your parents."

"Isn't it?" he said with his most charming smile. "I hope our visit hasn't caused too much trouble."

Molly batted her eyelashes. "No trouble at all."

Kelsey watched the exchange with interest. She didn't understand why Will's relationship to Molly bothered her. Kelsey may find him attractive. She may have kissed him. She may find him easy to talk with, too. But she wasn't interested in him. She didn't want to flirt with him or to date him. The only thing they had in common was planning Faith's wedding. If Molly could look beyond the band of gold on Will's finger, more power to her.

Will headed toward the samples. "Good thing we haven't eaten breakfast yet."

Molly laughed. "My portfolio is here if you want to

see some of the cakes I've made. There are lists of cake, filling and frosting combinations as well as paper and pencils to keep track of your tastings. I'll be in the kitchen if you have any questions.'' With that, she left.

"Look at all this cake.'' Will's eyes were wide as he pulled out a chair for Kelsey, then sat in another. "I don't know where to start.''

Kelsey knew exactly where she wanted to start. So she was a bit curious? It was only natural given how closely she was working with Will. "Do you know Molly well?''

"I've known her since she was a little kid.'' He grabbed a piece of chocolate cake with some sort of red filling. She glanced at her list. Must be the raspberry. "Hope baby-sat her.''

Kelsey picked up a piece of white chiffon cake with fudge filling. "So the Addisons and Fitzpatricks are old friends?''

"We go way back.'' He glanced up from his sample of cake. "Why do you ask?''

"It must have been a lot of work for her to go to so much trouble for you.''

"I've had women go to lots of trouble for me, but Molly isn't one of them.'' He laughed. "She didn't do all this for me. She did it for you.''

"Me?''

"You're the Wedding Consultant to the Stars.'' Will's laughter relaxed into a smile. "If you like her cakes, you might want to use her again. Why else do you think she agreed to bake a wedding cake at such short notice? She's in high demand around here.''

Duh. It was all Kelsey could do not to slap herself in the forehead. She felt like a complete moron. She was a professional wedding consultant, not his girlfriend, a jealous one at that. Kelsey took a deep breath. *Thank you, Will Addison, for turning me into a complete fool.*

He took a bite of a piece of chocolate. "This chocolate fudge is a slam dunk."

"Is that a good thing?"

"It's a very good thing."

"Don't eat it all." Chocolate always made things better. "I want a taste."

He broke off a piece and raised it to her mouth. She stared in his eyes, unsure for a moment.

"Open up," he said finally. "So you can taste it. This is how wedding cake was meant to be eaten."

She parted her lips. His fingers brushed her lips as he fed her the taste of cake. The gesture was so intimate, it took her a moment to remember to chew. But when she did... "This is incredible."

"I told you. But wait until you try this one." He fed her another piece. "What do you think?"

"Yummy." She picked up a sample of her own and took a bite. She penciled a few marks on her preference sheet. "This lemon melts in your mouth."

"Let me try."

Somehow her hand remained steady as she brought a piece to his lips and placed it into his mouth.

"This is so delicious." The look in his eyes made her wonder if he was talking about the cake or being fed. She wasn't sure of the difference herself. "Can I have another taste?" he asked.

Kelsey fed him another bite. He fed her. Back and forth. Again and again and again. They continued to feed each other the samples as if it were the most natural thing in the world. At that moment it felt natural and right and so many other wonderful things.

She couldn't explain it. She felt so comfortable with Will. Almost too comfortable for knowing him such a short time. Yet she could talk with him so easily. Open up and tell him things she'd only shared with family. Strange and disconcerting. Not to mention that kiss in the parking lot. Kelsey didn't even want to start thinking about that again.

Will reached over and brushed the edge of her mouth with his fingertip. "You have a little icing on your face."

"Thanks." The spot where he'd touched her radiated with heat. She ignored the urge to touch it, ignored the urge to lick the icing off his finger. Talk about jumping into the fire. She needed to stand back, way back, or she was going to get burned.

"So, do you have any favorites?" he asked.

Besides you? She swallowed hard. Focus. Focus on the task at hand. "I love the chocolate."

"Me, too."

"I also liked the lemon."

"Faith doesn't like lemon."

Kelsey felt as if he'd poured the pitcher of ice water on her face. She knew that about Faith. Why hadn't Kelsey remembered? It was her job to remember such details. But with Will around it was easy to forget what her job entailed. Much too easy. She had to be more careful. No flirting, not even a hint of it, and definitely no more kisses. "I forgot."

"The banana is pretty tasty."

"Yes, it is." Kelsey looked at two pictures in the baker's portfolio. If Molly combined the two designs, it would be perfect for the theme Kelsey had in mind. "We could order a three-tier cake. Two chocolate cakes and one banana."

"You know, I liked the lemon, too," Will admitted. "Why don't we do a three-tier cake, but sneak in the lemon? Faith will never know as long as we serve her a slice of one of the other cakes."

He really was something special. Kelsey smiled. "Sounds good to me."

Will ate the final bite of the remaining sample. "Tastes even better."

She stared at his mouth, the corners tipped up in a smile, and remembered the taste of his kiss.

But not as good as you.

Chapter Seven

February 6

Three days later Kelsey sat across from Will at his dining-room table. Scattered between them were file folders, notebooks, magazines, lists, sketches of the reception room, a phone book, a cell phone, a laptop and a Palm Pilot. The wedding plans were coming together.

"So, am I living up to your highly paid, highly qualified staff members?" Will asked.

She hesitated, long enough to make him sweat. "Your eyes aren't glassing over as much, which is quite an improvement."

"My eyes never glass over." She raised a brow, and he grinned sheepishly. "Maybe once or twice, but for someone who's never planned a wedding before, I'm doing great."

This she couldn't believe. Not after all he'd done for Faith's wedding. "What about your own wedding?"

"Sara knew what kind of wedding she wanted since the time she was twelve and took care of everything. I didn't do much except show up in a tux and say 'I do.'"

"Any regrets?"

"No. It was the wedding Sara wanted."

What did you want? The question was on the tip of Kelsey's tongue, but she managed to keep her curiosity from getting the best of her. More than once she'd felt her interest in Will go beyond client chitchat. Of course, their actions did, too. Kissing in the parking lot. Spending the night together on the couch. Feeding each other wedding cake. All those things went way beyond a business relationship. Yet it seemed right and normal, which made it even more odd. "So how does it feel?"

Will furrowed a brow. "How does what feel?"

"To finally plan a wedding?"

The edges of his mouth turned up slightly. "It's been...interesting."

Kelsey chuckled. "I suppose 'interesting' is a step above painful."

"I have to admit the cake tasting has been my favorite so far."

"Me, too."

Their gazes locked. She remembered staring into his eyes like this as she'd fed him a piece of cake, watching his lips close around her fingers as she pulled them—

Will looked away. "I'm learning a lot, though I don't know when I'll ever have the chance to use the knowledge again. So, where's the seating chart you've been working on?"

Kelsey rose, walked to his side of the table and placed two pieces of paper down. "What do you think?"

As he stared at the charts, Will's scent surrounded

her. Woodsy, spicy and oh-so-male. She felt a little dizzy and grabbed the edge of the table.

He touched her elbow. "You okay?"

"Fine."

"For a second you seemed to be in another world."

Yes, she realized, the land of good Will cologne. She let go of the edge. "I zoned out for a minute."

"You've been working too hard."

"*We've* been working too hard."

He smiled. She smiled back. "By the way, what's the name of the cologne you wear?"

"Cologne?"

"Is it aftershave?"

"I don't wear any."

"Oh." She gulped, feeling naked and exposed and oh-so embarrassed. "It's just Cade's birthday is coming up and..."

Will's eyes twinkled with amusement. "His birthday, huh?"

Busted. Heat flooded her already-warm cheeks. No problem, Kelsey told herself. It could be worse. She wasn't quite sure how, but... She cleared her Mojave-dry throat and nodded.

He stared at her, a wry smile on his lips. "Which one am I supposed to look at?"

"Which one what?"

"Which seating chart?"

"Both of them."

What was happening to her? Embarrassing herself was one thing, but acting like a total airhead was another. So what if Will smelled good and it wasn't man-made but his own natural scent and maybe a nice bar of soap or even his shampoo? So what if he knew she liked how he smelled, too? No big deal. She could ignore it. Ignore that her new standard of what a man should smell like had just been cemented in her mind and olfactory nerves.

"Why are there two?" he asked.

"One is for the wedding reception and one is for the anniversary party."

Will flashed her a here-we-go-again look, then studied the chart. "This is really detailed."

"The last thing you want are any big surprises on the big day so I try to be as detailed as possible to see how things will mesh."

"Is that why you were trying on the veil?"

"What veil?"

"At your office." Interest gleamed in Will's gaze. "You say you don't want to be a bride yourself, yet you tried on the veil. Why?"

"I wanted to see if the veil and wreath matched."

"Couldn't you have just held them up together?"

Yes, but she hadn't. Kelsey wasn't sure what had compelled her to try them on, but she wasn't about to admit that to Will. He already knew too much about her. She was a private person, but something made it easy for her to open up to him. But not about this. She tilted her chin. "I wanted to see the full effect."

"And did you?"

"I did." She'd seen a whole lot more than that, too. It was if she'd been transported to another time, another place. Everything she'd never expected to feel—love, happily-ever-after, magic—had filled her office for that one moment. Her lips trembled with the urge to smile, but she didn't. "Just part of the job."

He studied her, his eyes cool and contemplative. "It always comes back to the job."

"A wedding is serious business to the bride and

groom.'' Very serious, Kelsey realized. She couldn't afford to be distracted by foolish romantic notions and Will Addison. Strictly business. That's all her relationship could be, all she wanted it to be. "Wait until you see the schedule I'm putting together. Talk about detailed. Timing makes or breaks a wedding reception. If it's right, no one will notice, but if it's off, guests know."

"I don't get it." Will raised a brow. "How can you put so much work into a wedding you don't think will last let alone happen in the first place?"

The way he looked at her made Kelsey feel as if she were disappointing him, and it bothered her. His feelings about her shouldn't—make that, didn't—matter to her. "I agreed to coordinate Faith's wedding, and I'm doing it. What I believe about the situation doesn't enter into it."

"Situation?" His eyes darkened. "We're talking about two people who love each other and plan to spend the rest of their lives together."

"We're talking about two people who'll be lucky to make it to the 'I do' so don't even start in on happily-ever-after."

Kelsey's gaze locked with his. Stalemate.

It was bound to happen over and over again. Their beliefs were too different. But that didn't explain the heavy feeling in her stomach.

She pointed to the charts. "Tell me what you think."

Will studied both of the seating arrangements. "Don't seat Uncle Wayne so close to the bar, and make sure Hope and her kids are near an exit."

Kelsey scribbled a note on the anniversary seating chart. She wouldn't need the other one. "That was too easy."

"How hard can it be to seat forty-eight people?"

"You don't want to know. Between the bride and groom, their friends and families." A warning sounded in her head. "Have you mentioned any of our plans to Faith and Trent?"

"No," Will said. "Faith doesn't want to be disturbed during filming. I'm doing exactly what she wants me to do, and a good job of it if I do say so myself."

"What about Trent?"

"If it mattered to him, he'd be the one overseeing the wedding plans instead of me."

"What does that say about your future-brother-in-law?"

"He's a lot smarter than me." Will grinned. "Don't worry. Faith will call if she has any concerns."

He sounded so nonchalant, as if they were planning a surprise birthday party, not a wedding. Relaxed was one thing, but this...

What-ifs swirled in her head. What if Faith hated the wedding? What if Trent hated it more? What if Faith didn't even show up? Kelsey took a deep breath. "I wasn't really worried before. A little concerned, but now..."

Will gave her hand a gentle squeeze. "Everything is fine. Faith trusts me. And you."

The only problem was, Kelsey didn't trust herself. Not with Will around.

"Thank you," Kelsey said to the operator at the San Montico palace. Waiting for her call to be transferred to the royal suite, she shifted the phone to her left ear and laid on her bed. It was only noon, but she was tired. Kelsey wiggled her toes inside her wool socks to keep her blood flowing. A little energy was all she needed to get through the rest of the day.

She had to admit she missed having her staff, but Will was doing the best he could for a guy clueless about the ongoings of a wedding. He had a lot of connections and contacts in the Lake Tahoe/Reno area. From arranging security to transporting guests from the inn to the ceremony and back to the reception, they had accomplished more than she thought possible this morning. But so much work awaited them, work they would do together.

The more time Kelsey spent with Will, the better she got to know him. She liked what she was learning, too. He was a hard worker. He was also devoted to his family. And what a family. Will might say his family wasn't perfect, but they were as perfect a family as she'd ever seen. She enjoyed being with his parents, too, even if it was only a brief stop to update Starr and Bill on the progress of the wedding plans. With parents like that, Kelsey couldn't blame him for his views on love and marriage and happily-ever-after, but it was a red flag to her and all she knew to be true.

Forget about how good he smelled or how good a man he appeared to be or how good he made her feel. His beliefs threatened her own. Any temptation to let her heart decide what to do about Will Addison was not allowed, not even for a moment.

She had to forget about his kisses, his kindness, his warmth.

She had to stop thinking of him as anything other than the brother of the bride, the person who was helping her coordinate Faith Starr's wedding.

Bottom line: Kelsey enjoyed his company and appreciated his input. She had to admit they made a pretty good team. But it didn't—couldn't—go further than that. As soon as the wedding was over...

"Hello?" The familiar voice of her cousin, Christina, came across the line as if they were in the same room. She didn't sound a continent and an ocean away.

Kelsey smiled. "I hope I didn't wake you, Princess."

"I was just getting ready for bed."

"A little early, don't you think? It's only nine over there."

"I said bed," Christina replied. "Not sleep."

"Touché. Your message sounded strange." With her fingertip, Kelsey traced one of the flowers on the floral-patterned duvet cover. "What's up?"

"Well..."

The way Christina's voice faded worried Kelsey. She sat up. "Is everything okay?"

Silence.

Oh, boy. This could only mean one thing—marital problems. Kelsey scooted off the bed. But that didn't make any sense. Christina and Richard were the perfect couple. Meant—no, destined—to be together. If they couldn't make their marriage work, there was no hope for anyone else. Kelsey paced back and forth until she couldn't take it any longer. "Are you and Richard—"

"We're fine."

Thank goodness. She exhaled the breath she'd been holding. "What's going on, Christina?"

"I wanted to tell you in person, but the press has been sniffing around and since you aren't coming..."

If it wasn't Christina's marriage, what could it be? Uncle Alan? Aunt Claire? Kelsey was losing her patience. Damn high-tech phone. Where was a cord to twirl when you needed one most? "Tell me. Now."

"You're going to be a godmother."

"A godmother?" Kelsey wet her lips. "I don't understand."

"I'm pregnant," Christina blurted. "With twins."

"Twins?" Excitement mixed with surprise. Feeling a bit light-headed, Kelsey sat. She missed the bed and hit the ground with a thud.

"Are you okay?" Christina asked.

Okay? Kelsey was more than okay. She laughed, and her heart swelled with joy. "I'm fine except next time you have good news like that, Princess, make sure I'm sitting down first."

That evening Will carried in a box of food his mother had delivered from the inn. As he placed the box on the kitchen counter, he noticed an expensive bottle of champagne tucked inside. Leave it to his mother. "Just great."

Kelsey glanced up from her notebook. Her eyes clouded with concern. "Is something wrong?"

He hoped his mother would come to her senses over the letter she'd written. Obviously she hadn't, and now she was taking things into her own hands. What a joke. Mom didn't know Kelsey as well as he did, otherwise she would never be trying to push them together. Two people couldn't be less suitable for each other than he and Kelsey. Not that he didn't enjoy her company. He did. A lot. "My mother's trying to play matchmaker."

"Excuse me?"

He pulled out the bottle. Nicely chilled and ready to be opened. And Kelsey said he had nothing to worry about. To think she thought his family was perfect. What a laugh. "Look what came with our dinner."

"Your mother didn't order it, I did."

"You did?"

Kelsey nodded.

Images of an empty bottle of champagne, an uneaten dinner left cooling on the table and Kelsey sent his temperature rising. Forget about his mother. He had a bigger problem. Himself. Will cleared his dry throat. "Why champagne?"

"I wanted to celebrate."

"Celebrate?"

She nodded, pulled out two crystal champagne flutes from the box and batted her long, luscious eyelashes. "Care to join me?"

A smile lit up her face. A smile directed straight at him. This could only mean...

Oh, hell. She wasn't celebrating. She was propositioning him. He should have known this would happen. It always did. No matter how hard women might say they weren't interested in him. They couldn't help themselves. Not even Kelsey.

Let her down easy, he told himself. Don't make a big deal out of it. But no words would come. He simply stared at her, an odd mix of apprehension and anticipation duking it out inside of him.

She rose from the table and walked toward him. The sway of her hips seemed more noticeable. Her complexion glowed. And her eyes. It was as if a million stars had sprung to life in their depths. A ripple of excitement rushed through him.

She picked up the champagne bottle. "There should be a chocolate cake in there from Molly Fitzpatrick, too."

And oysters for appetizers? How was he going to get out of this? Not that he wasn't tempted. He was. More than he should be. But thinking and doing were two totally different things. And what about the wedding they still needed to plan?

If anything happened...nothing would. Nothing could. She didn't believe in anything he did. Not love or marriage or happily-ever-after. Not that he was looking for any of those things. He wasn't, and she wasn't, Will realized. Did that mean she was only after one night? His pulse pounded in his throat.

She held the bottle and dried the neck with a towel. Back and forth. Back and forth. Will swallowed. Hard.

"Of course," she said, her voice seductive, "we'll have to wait until we eat this delicious-smelling dinner first before we cut into dessert."

His gaze focused on her full lips. Desire hit him low and hard. It was as if Kelsey had flicked on a switch Will hadn't known existed. Forget about cake, he wanted...

"We could eat dessert first." The words slipped out of his mouth. What was he doing? Thinking? Becoming? He brushed his hand through his hair.

Her grin widened. She unwrapped the foil and twisted the wire covering the cork. The bottle opened with a pop, and he thought he was going to pop himself. "I like how you think."

I like how you think, too. And so much more than that. Trouble, he was in big trouble. Slow down. Forget she's a woman. Yeah, right. He'd have to be in a coma.

Maybe this wasn't so bad, after all. He wasn't looking for forever; neither was she.

Kelsey filled the glasses, handed one to him and raised her own. "To the future members of the de Thierry royal family."

"To..." Will was about to say, "To us." He felt as light-headed as the bubbles rising in the champagne. "What did you say?"

"My cousin, Christina, is pregnant and asked me to be the babies' godmother."

He blinked, trying to clear his head. She had to mean, "Oh, baby" not— "Babies?"

"Twins, actually." Kelsey grinned. "An heir and a spare according to Christina."

He stared at her, confused.

"But Christina said this is still hush-hush so please don't tell anyone."

"And we're celebrating her pregnancy?"

"Yes. I'm going to throw her a shower. Maybe two. One in San Montico, the other in Chicago. There will be so much to buy. Two of everything. Little dresses and dolls if she has girls. Footballs and trucks if she has boys. Maybe she'll have one of each. That would be perfect. I still can't believe she's having twins, and I'm going to be their godmother. That's such a big deal. I'll be Aunt Kelsey. An aunt. I never thought I'd be an aunt. Cade's not planning to get married and have kids. I'll have to knit booties and little caps. I think that's what aunts and godmothers do. But I don't know how to knit. No matter, I'll figure it out." She stopped rambling and stared at him. Her cheeks reddened. "Sorry I went on like that, but I'm pretty excited. Was there something else—"

"No," he answered quickly, and tried to make sense of it all. This was about babies not baby-making. It took a moment for the truth to set in, and another moment for the disappointment to wash over him. Kelsey wasn't after him. She wasn't trying to seduce him. Will had only one question on his mind. Why not?

What now?

The celebration over Christina's pregnancy had taken

a strange turn of events, and Kelsey was confused. Very confused.

Meaningful glances and seductive smiles and an accidental brush of Will's hand that became a tender touch. He couldn't be coming on to her, yet she couldn't explain his actions over dinner. Mind games, overreaction, too much champagne?

Too much bubbly was the easy answer.

But now as she stood at the trailhead across from the inn's service entrance waiting for Will to return from inside, Kelsey knew it wasn't the champagne. She had only herself to blame for letting him get under her skin.

Will had done nothing to fuel her fantasies but be himself. He couldn't help it if everything he did and said appealed to her on a level she never knew existed.

It had to end.

Kelsey might have told herself to keep it strictly business, but she struggled with the task. She needed to put all these fantasies to rest once and for all. And she knew right where to start...

With his kiss.

She wanted to kiss Will. No, she corrected herself, she needed to kiss him. She wanted to prove to herself there was nothing between them. No chemistry, no attraction, nothing. That was the first step to stopping this foolishness.

It had been days ago, but she could close her eyes and still taste him, feel him. Never before had a kiss that meant so little felt like so much. And she wanted a repeat performance. She wanted to prove this mythic-proportion memory was all in her mind. That his kiss wasn't so spectacular, after all.

"The coast is clear."

Kelsey jumped at the sound of Will's voice. Talk

about having her head in the clouds. She hadn't even seen him approaching.

"You okay?" he asked.

No, she wasn't okay, but she still nodded. This was bad. She couldn't let it go any further. She had to kiss him. Tonight. Asking for permission didn't appeal to her in the slightest. She wasn't the begging type. Trying to explain the situation was not going to happen. She had her pride. Stealing a kiss was the only way to go. But how?

He squeezed her shoulder. "Cold?"

She stared into his eyes. Will's gaze lingered, practically caressed. A slow heat burned its way through her. She'd never felt more feminine, more desirable, in all her life. This was her chance. *Get it over with. Kiss him now so you can start forgetting about him.* "N-no."

"Come on, the chef is expecting us."

As she followed Will across the slush-covered pavement, she noticed a few hotel guests exiting the lobby and milling about the main entrance. She remembered the last time she'd seen people coming out of the inn. It might work again. It *had* to work again.

"Reporters," she whispered, crossing her fingers behind her back.

Will turned. Before he could say anything she wrapped her arms around him. The nearness of him overwhelmed her. Too bad, she had to get this over with so she could focus her attention on Faith's wedding.

"Kiss me." Kelsey forced the word from her dry throat, and hoped she didn't sound as desperate as she felt. As she raised her lips to meet his, she told herself what to feel—nothing. One kiss and then...

Will's lips touched hers. His kiss was as light as a

snowflake. Sweet. Okay, she could deal with this. Nice and pleasant, too. Nothing to write home about. Relief washed over her, and she smiled. Now she could get on with the wedding planning and put all this behind her. Kelsey parted her lips to say, "Stop," but she never got the word out.

Will deepened the kiss, pressing his lips against hers with a hunger that both surprised and flattered her. Kiss after kiss after kiss.

The snowflake turned into a blizzard. A total white-out. Kelsey couldn't see; she didn't care. She only wanted to feel Will's warmth, his strength, and soak up the taste of him—champagne and chocolate and something uniquely his own.

Kelsey was caught in an avalanche of sensation, but she wanted to do more than go along for the ride. She leaned into him, met his kiss with a hunger all her own. As his tongue explored the recesses of her mouth, she did the same with an eagerness so unfamiliar to her. Pleasure pulsated within her, and she quivered.

Will pulled her toward him. She met him halfway, and his arms tightened around her. So strong, so warm, so right.

Her entire life she'd longed for permanence and stability and family. She found the promise of all three in Will's arms. Each touch of his hands and his lips shattered everything she'd come to believe over the years. Happily-ever-after. With him. Maybe it was…possible.

He ran his hands down her back, along the curve of her waist and cupped her bottom. Will pulled her closer, as close as their jackets and clothing allowed. She pressed against him, her body melting against his. She moaned, relishing the feel and texture of him.

Will dragged the kiss to an end, but kept his arms

around her and his face next to hers. His own breath, ragged and hot, fanned her temple. "Are they gone?" he whispered.

She tried to steady her uneven breaths. Her heart hammered in her ears. Her lips ached for more kisses. "Who?"

"The reporters."

Her pulse went from supersonic speed to a dead stop. Like a snowball hitting her square on the face and breaking her nose, the reality of what she'd done made her stagger backward. She glanced around, not able to focus on anything, not even Will. "I don't see them."

"That means they didn't see us." He smiled. "Quick thinking."

The last thing she deserved was praise of any kind. She wanted to crawl into the nearest hole.

He slipped his hand around hers, and she nearly gasped. "We'd better keep up the appearance just in case."

"O-okay." She forced the word out.

Talk about making a situation worse. Not only had she lied about seeing reporters, she'd gotten more than she bargained for with the second kiss—make that kisses. This kiss was nothing like the first. At least she'd been right about that. Too bad this kiss was better, monumentally better. And now they were walking into the inn hand-in-hand, as if they were a couple. The worst part was, it felt totally natural. Kelsey suppressed a groan.

Somebody just shoot her now. It would be the easiest way out.

Chapter Eight

February 7

The next morning he opened a can of food for Midas, and the cat came running as fast as his three legs would carry him. Will dished the food onto a plate and mashed it with a fork.

A kiss, he rationalized. That's all it had been, a kiss. Nothing more, nothing less. No reason to beat himself up over it and lose another night's sleep tossing and turning over it. He'd kissed other women before. He would kiss other women after.

After Kelsey.

A heaviness centered in his chest, squeezed his already-aching heart. Up till now it had always been after Sara. Up till now...

Maybe he was lonely. Maybe his mother was right about that. Maybe that explained all of this. Working too hard, traveling too much, not getting out and socializing enough. He stared down at Midas. "It's been me and you for so long, I forgot how nice it was to have another person to talk with. Not that I don't like talking to you, but Kelsey..."

Midas glanced up from his dish and meowed.

Will rubbed him, then fed him a forkful of food. "I like her, too."

Like, he repeated to himself. Not anything more. He couldn't let it go further than that. Unfortunately that didn't explain what was happening.

Longing and desire. Feelings that had lain dormant for so long were springing to life, thawing his frozen heart in the middle of winter. All of the feelings had one thing in common. All of them surrounded Kelsey Armstrong Waters.

The out-of-this-world kiss last night that he hadn't want to end. The way her hand fit so snugly, so perfectly, in his that he hadn't wanted to let go. The meeting with the chef that had made him feel as if he and Kelsey were the couple getting married not the pair simply planning the wedding.

The wedding. Faith's wedding.

Will was beginning to imagine Kelsey as the bride and himself as the groom. It had to stop. The fantasy forming in his mind had replaced memories of his own wedding with Sara.

A silver-dollar-size lump of guilt lodged in his throat. Guilt over having such a good time with Kelsey. Guilt over wanting to kiss her again and again. Guilt over putting Kelsey in Sara's place.

No, Will corrected himself, where Sara was and would be.

Today, tomorrow, always.

Nothing would ever change that. Nothing could.

Yet these feelings for Kelsey aren't going away, a quiet voice in his head reminded him. Did it matter?

Not in the long run.

Whatever feelings he might have for her were temporary, like the traffic on a three-day holiday weekend after a good snowfall. All would be back to normal come Tuesday. The same would happen here.

Will's life would be back to normal come February fifteenth. The battle between what he thought was right and what he felt was right would end in a draw. The wedding would be over, Faith would be a married woman and Kelsey would be long gone, back to Beverly Hills and her dysfunctional family. Back to designing weddings and looking for unhappy endings.

Not his problem, he told himself. She was a capable adult. He didn't need to play white knight to her misguided heart. She would figure it out on her own when the time was right. He couldn't do anything about it.

Not even kiss her until she saw the light.

February 8

Light reflected off the heart-shaped silver frame that Kelsey held in the air. She was putting her foot down about this, even if it went against Starr's wishes. "No engraving."

"We're discussing minutia." Will rubbed the back of his neck. "It's only a frame."

"First, it's not only a frame." Kelsey placed it on the table. "It's going to be used as a place card holder at the reception."

"Who cares?"

"I care, and your mother cares." She understood why both of them were edgy. Late nights, little sleep, lots of work. Not to mention her growing attraction for Will. That alone was enough to make her skin clammy, her stomach clench and her heart pound like the bass drum in a marching band. Anxiety attack? Or an ulcer? Maybe Will had succeeded where his sister had failed. Kelsey pushed her hair behind her ears. "We need to make a decision or we'll run out of time and it'll be made for us."

Will rubbed the stubble on his chin. He hadn't shaved today. Normally Kelsey only found clean-shaven men attractive—George Clooney excluded—but Will's stubble gave him a rugged, earthly appeal. She wondered if it would tickle if it scraped her skin.

"Buy forty-eight more," he suggested. "You can always return them."

"I don't want the frames engraved. Period."

For the first time in hours, amusement flickered in Will's eyes. The corners of his mouth tipped upward.

"What?" she asked.

"You sound like a bride."

"No, I don't," she said the words quickly, too quickly.

"Yes, you do." Will edged forward in his chair. "That's why every tiny detail has been discussed to death and taken a major peace accord to decide. These frames—excuse me, place card holders—are the prime example. You sound exactly like a bride who doesn't want to do what her future mother-in-law wants her to do."

He should know better than to tease her about this. He knew how she felt about weddings and being a bride herself. Kelsey swallowed around the lump of disappointment in her throat.

"I don't—" Realization dawned, and the protest died

on her lips. Kelsey's jaw dropped. "I sound like a bride. A bride."

Will chuckled. "It's not that bad."

"Oh, yes, it is. It's worse than bad. It's horrendous."

"It's kind of cute actually."

"It's nothing of the sort." What was happening to her? With her fingertips rubbing her temples, she rose from her chair. "In case you haven't noticed, I'm totally freaked out by this."

"I wouldn't say totally." His grin widened. "At least, not yet."

"And I thought you were a nice guy." She paced back and forth. "This can't be happening. A bride is the last thing I ever want to be. I'm a wedding consultant. A professional."

"You are a professional."

"I was, but at the moment..." She blew out a puff of air. It didn't do any good. "I'm supposed to be doing my job, not getting carried away as if I were planning my own wedding." The blood drained from her face, and she stopped. "Do you think I'm turning into a bride wanna-be?"

Laughter poured from Will. He wiped the corner of his eye. "Trust me, Kelsey, the last thing you'll ever be is a bride wanna-be."

"Thank you." She took a calming breath. "I was hoping I hadn't, but I really needed to hear someone else say it."

"No problem." He rose, put his hands on her shoulders and led her back to her chair. "Sit."

Kelsey did, and Will kneaded her shoulders. "You're so tense. Relax for a minute."

His touch made her stiffen. She didn't want his hands on her. What if she really liked it? She was already acting as though this was *her* wedding. Would she start planning the honeymoon next? "Easier said than done."

"Try."

"Okay." Her muscles were tight and knotted, but Will didn't stop. Slowly, ever so slowly, his skillful hands worked their magic, loosening the kinks. As he continued the massage, all of the tension seemed to flow out of her and evaporate. She'd never felt anything like it. She wanted to lay her head down and melt into the dining table.

"Relaxed?" he asked.

"Uh-huh."

"Close your eyes."

They were already closed, but she wasn't about to spoil the moment. He massaged the back of her neck and moved up, his hands in her hair.

"I want you to start over," he said softly. "I want you to tell me about the frames now that you have some distance. Can you do that?"

As long as he kept touching her this way she could do anything. Kelsey nodded.

"Now," he prompted.

With her eyes still closed, she took a breath. "We need to make a decision about engraving the place card holders."

"Tell me why we shouldn't engrave them."

He was doing amazing things with her scalp and hair. Those hands of his, those remarkable hands. She sighed.

"Tell me why?" he repeated.

"If Faith doesn't show up, we can use them for the anniversary party."

He removed his hands. "See."

She opened her eyes. "See what?"

"You're back."

Kelsey sat still for a moment and waited. No errant thoughts came to her head. No emotional reasons for any decision to be made. No sign of bridal anxiety. "Thank you."

"Anytime." He motioned the silver heart on the table. "So the frames..."

"If they're engraved, the frames will join the rest of Faith's and her groom du jour's cache of engraved favors—five hundred fish bowls, four hundred bottles of champagne and flutes, three hundred sand castles, two hundred gold snuff boxes and another two hundred silver tussie-mussies."

"Tussie-mussies?"

"It's from the Regency period, Jane Austin times, and shaped like a cone. Ladies used them to hold their hand-tied flower bouquets at balls. Each flower had a symbolic meaning—"

"More information than I need or want to know."

"You asked." Kelsey, the wedding designer, was back; Kelsey, the overstressed bride, was gone. That wasn't about to happen again. She tilted her chin. "And now I'm asking. You know what I want, you know what your mother wants. You have the casting vote."

Will sat in his chair across the table from Kelsey. "I abstain."

"Not an option."

His brows drew together. "Engrave the date on the frames and leave off the names."

"I can live with that. Date on frame, no names." Kelsey jotted a note on one of her many lists. She glanced up at Will. "You make a fine mediator."

"It's a skill you need with two younger sisters." He

leaned back in his chair. "Any more decisions we need to make today?"

She checked her list. "No, but we need to start work on the favors. We can set up on the end of the table."

"Wait a minute." A lock of hair fell across his forehead, and he brushed it back. Kelsey wished she could have been the one—no, she didn't. "Aren't the frames the favors?"

"No." She opened a manila folder marked with a giant heart to symbolize a favor. Starr had a unique way of labeling her files. "They're the place card holders, remember?"

Will rubbed his eyes. "Why don't we ask Faith and Trent to do us a favor and elope?"

Kelsey did a double take. "I don't believe you said that."

"Neither do I," Will admitted as much to his surprise as hers. "Blame it on an overdose of bridal magazines and wedding planning. A man can only take so much."

She wadded up a piece of paper and tossed it at his head. Will caught it midair.

"Good catch," she said. "Now, about the favors. We're going to decorate and fill heart-shaped boxes with a hand-blown glass heart, chocolate truffles and a Valentine's card."

"'We'?"

He sounded as if she'd asked him to wear a pair of tights and a pink tutu. She suppressed a laugh. "It won't be so bad."

"Doesn't that depend on your definition of 'bad?' I didn't even make any of the favors for my own wedding."

She was really looking forward to this. Kelsey

grinned. "You're going to have lots of fun with the hot glue gun."

"Hot glue and fun." Will grimaced. "I've never connected the two before."

"Oh, you will." Kelsey winked. "Trust me on this one. You will."

February 11

How had this happened?

Three days later, Will stood in his dining room. With the favor-making supplies set up at one end of the dining-room table and the wedding-planning paraphernalia at the other, it was a guy's worst nightmare. And he was living it—twenty-four seven.

An hour of using a hot glue gun and fumbling with ribbons and bows and heart-shaped boxes was all he could take. A man had only so much patience. And his hands were too damn big. So they compromised. Kelsey would work on the favors by herself, and he would run all the errands and make all the phone calls.

He heard a meow. Midas sat on the back of a chair staring out a window into the backyard. Will walked toward him. "What do you see boy? A bird?"

Another meow.

He glanced out the window and saw what had captured Midas's attention. Kelsey stood with her head tilted back, catching snowflakes on her tongue. She hadn't worn a hat. Her long hair swung about her back. He loved her hair especially when she wore it down.

"Meow is right." Will patted Midas's head and watched Kelsey. She looked so happy and carefree as she played out in the snow. Her smile showed how much she was enjoying herself. "Be right back."

Will pulled on his jacket and stepped outside. The scent of pine and tree sap hung in the chilly air, reminding him of Christmastime and chopping down the family tree as they did every year. "Did you get tired of making favors?"

She glanced over at him. "When the snow started falling, I decided to take a break."

"All the errands and calls are done."

"Good for you." She spread her arms out and twirled. With all her hair and a lavender scarf for wings, she looked like a snow fairy. "I'm not even close to being done."

"You don't sound too worried."

"It'll get done."

She sounded so unlike her normally organized, on-top-of-everything self. "Are you okay?"

"I'm better than okay. I'm in heaven. Look at all of this. I've never seen so many trees. You can taste the green. And those mountains. Have you ever seen anything so stunning as those snowcapped peaks? And this snow." Kelsey picked up a handful of snow and tossed it in the air above her. Her laughter bubbled over and surrounded his heart. "It's so fresh and white. You can almost smell it. I never realized that before."

Her enthusiasm was contagious. Will grinned. "You need to get out of L.A. if a simple snowfall will have this effect."

"You may be right." She smiled. "But it brings back so many memories. I used to love playing in the snow. Cade and I would stay outdoors until we couldn't stand the cold any longer. We'd have snowball fights, make snowmen and snow angels—you name it. You must have loved growing up here."

"I did."

As the tip of her tongue darted out and caught another snowflake, Will felt a twinge in his groin. Damn. He had to get a grip. Nothing had changed between them; nothing was going to change between them. A few more days and she would be out of his life. The prospect didn't seem as appealing as it once had.

She spun around again. "All of this in your own backyard... Tell me what it was like to be a kid here. The skiing, the sledding. It had to be incredible."

"It was great. And not only in the wintertime. We played out here year-long." He walked toward a patch of trees. The snow wet the cuffs of his pants. "Didn't matter what the weather or the season. My mother dressed us accordingly. She was an expert at getting us out the door with minimal hassle. My sisters and I used to have huge snowball fights in the winter, water fights in the summer." He motioned to a clearing beyond the trees. "That was Yankee Stadium, Wimbledon and Hollywood all rolled into one."

"Active imaginations."

Smiling, he nodded. "It was better than watching TV all day, but we did end up with more than our fair share of bumps, bruises and broken appendages."

"You and your sisters?"

"Me and Hope," he admitted. "The only thing that ever happened to Faith was a dog bite from a guest's pet. You can still see the scar if you know where to look."

"Your poor mother." A snowflake landed on Kelsey's nose, and she brushed it off. "She must have had her hands full with the bumps and bruises and broken bones and dog bites."

"Don't forget the blood." Will grinned, remembering his mother's resigned sigh each time something happened to one of them. "There was lots of blood and trips to the emergency room when we were growing up."

"More credit to Starr." Kelsey set out making a snowman. "Good thing I don't plan on having kids because I wouldn't be able to handle all of that. I get dizzy at the sight of ketchup."

He chuckled. "I'm sure you'll figure it out."

"I won't need to figure it out." She patted a ball of snow together. "Trust me, I'm better off with no plants, no pets and no kids."

"You can't be serious."

"I am."

He stared at her as if seeing her for the first time. Silence stretched between them. "But you were so excited about your cousin's pregnancy. Throwing two showers, buying baby things, knitting booties even though you don't know how to knit. That doesn't sound as if you don't like kids."

"I never said I didn't like kids. I do. I love other people's kids. You can spoil them rotten and then give them back," she admitted. "It's too easy to screw them up when they're your own."

A pain squeezed his heart at the thought of her never having a baby of her own. "That's too bad because you'd be a wonderful mother."

Kelsey dropped the snowball and it splattered on the ground. Her startled gaze met his. "Me? A wonderful mother?"

The incredulous tone of her voice brought a smile to his face. Kelsey might not think she was mother material, but she was. "I've seen you with Midas. You've got the touch."

"Midas is a cat."

"Doesn't matter. Whether you believe it or not, you've got the mothering instinct like my sister Hope had when we were growing up. You'll see what a great mother she turned out to be when she arrives for the wedding with her family." As he walked toward Kelsey, she took a step back. No matter. Will wasn't about to let her dismiss something so important. "With all you went through growing up, you wouldn't make the same mistakes as your parents made. I know you wouldn't."

"That's so nice of you to say." Gratitude glimmered in Kelsey's eyes and filled him with a comforting warmth. "Thank you."

"You're welcome." One end of her scarf was dragging on the ground. He wrapped it around her. "So you might not want to be so quick to give up on love and marriage and happily-ever-after."

She glanced downward. "It isn't going to work."

"What?"

"You can't change my entire belief system with one compliment."

"I wasn't trying to." He raised her chin with his fingertip. "What I meant to say was, any kid would be lucky to have you for a mother. It would be a big loss if that didn't happen someday. Emphasis on the someday."

He said that as much for his own benefit as hers.

Gazing into her eyes, he felt a sense of completeness as if a missing gap had suddenly been filled. But of all the women in the world, how could it be this one? One that was so different from—

"I wish I could believe…"

"You can." He caressed her cheek, gently tracing a

line down to her chin with his fingertip. "Believe, Kelsey. Believe."

She parted her lips, but he didn't give her the chance to speak. He covered her mouth with his own.

So sweet. Melt-in-your-mouth sweet, like cotton candy.

He wasn't sure why he kissed her, but it was the smartest move he'd made all week next to getting out of the favor making. Hell, if she kept kissing him this way he might give the old glue gun another try. And the ribbons.

Her hands splayed across his back, pulling him closer. He went willingly, without a nanosecond of hesitation. He tasted snow and Kelsey and something else, something exotic, a forbidden fruit or magic potion or enchanted elixir. The tastes mingled, blended. Temptation, desire and romance. He couldn't forget the romance. That was the most important part. He only needed to make Kelsey see it, feel it, believe it.

As she leaned into him, into the kiss, he wound his left hand in her hair. The soft hair sifted through his fingers like strands of silk. Now this was heaven, and he didn't want it to end.

The snowflurries picked up and circled them. He felt as if they'd stepped into a winter wonderland snow globe. His only wish was that as soon as the music stopped someone would wind the key so they could start again. And again. And again.

Will didn't care that everything he'd thought, everything he'd believed, was flying out the door faster than candy on Halloween. He'd care later. He'd bet Starr Properties' newest resort in the Bahamas that he'd care a lot, but not now. Not at this perfect moment.

This wasn't a mere kiss. Kelsey wasn't a mere woman.

He kissed her again and again. She kissed him back again and again. She sighed, a quiet-as-a-whisper-sigh that spoke volumes. His blood roared through his veins. He was king of the jungle, king of the world. Her lips pressed against his once again. Searching, seeking, finding…

He wanted her. He wanted her more than he'd ever wanted—

Will tore away from her.

Eyes wide and her breathing ragged, she stared at him. A faint blush reddened her cheeks. It wasn't from the cold. Not this time. "I—"

"No, I—"

"I'm sorry."

"I'm the one who's sorry," he apologized, but the last thing he felt was sorry. "I started it."

She stared into his eyes. "I didn't stop you."

I should have stopped myself. But he couldn't say the words out loud. Because, heaven help him, he hadn't wanted to stop. Not then, not even now. He'd wanted more, all she had to give him.

And it scared Will, downright terrified him. He couldn't remember feeling so out of control with Sara. Maybe he'd forgotten. He'd been carrying memories of her with him for so long. But that didn't make the way he was feeling right.

"Don't beat yourself up over this," Kelsey said. "You didn't do anything wrong."

Will couldn't look her in the eyes. It was as if she could read his mind. How could someone he'd known for such a short time know him so well? It was all so very…strange. Yet felt so very right. Almost too right.

She combed her gloved fingers through her tousled and tangled hair. "Chalk it up to the heat of the moment."

"It's freezing out here." Of course, he was sweating. And he wasn't wearing a hat or gloves.

"So it was the chill of the moment. Same difference." She grinned. "I think I see the beginnings of a smile." The edges of his mouth curled upward. "Oh, yes. There it is."

"Do you want to talk about...this?"

She stared at him with disbelief. "Isn't that supposed to be my line?"

"Yes, but you're also the one who should be the die-hard romantic, not me."

"Touché." She went to work on her snowman. "There's not much to discuss. We kissed. It's over. And we shouldn't do it again."

"Shouldn't do what again?"

"Kiss."

He might have been thinking the exact same thing, but he hadn't expected her to say it. "You didn't like it?"

"I liked it," she admitted, much to his relief. "But it isn't going anywhere—we aren't, I mean. We're so different. Too different. And the wedding's right around the corner. That has to be the priority. We can't be distracted."

"Do I distract you, Kelsey?"

"Sometimes. But your kisses really distract me." She flipped her hair behind her shoulder. "Do you understand what I'm getting at?"

Will wasn't certain. He wasn't certain about anything right now, which told him exactly what needed to be said. Kelsey was right. "No more kisses."

She nodded. "No more kisses."

Chapter Nine

February 12

The next day Kelsey sat at the kitchen table and stared out the window at the glistening snow covering the ground.

She rubbed her tired eyes. She should be asleep not sitting here thinking about kisses and babies and Will. But that's exactly what she was doing and had done most of last night.

No more kisses.

Yesterday, Will's kiss had her standing on the edge of heaven, on the edge of hell. She couldn't be certain which. All she knew was that it had felt good and right and the way it was meant to be between a man and a woman. Self-preservation had her trying to keep herself from careening over the edge. Telling Will they shouldn't kiss again seemed like the easiest way. It would be easier to stop drinking water or even breathing. She touched her trembling lips with a fingertip. She could still feel his kiss, his warmth, him.

You'd be a wonderful mother.

Will had blown her away with his compliment. She never wanted to put any child through what she had gone through growing up, but her aversion went deeper than that. She never planned to marry, and she truly believed with all her heart a child deserved two parents who loved each other and lived together and were married. Will would probably laugh at her traditional view of family, but she didn't care. That's how she felt, and that's why she would remain single with no kids. It had always been what she wanted. It was the life she enjoyed. So why was it suddenly not enough? Why did the thought of having a baby seem so appealing all of a sudden?

Will.

Will and his family of pure romantics.

That's the only explanation. All of their happily-ever-after, one-love-in-a-lifetime mumbo-jumbo was messing with her brain. A part of her wanted to believe, but she couldn't close her eyes to the reality of marriage—infidelity, unhappiness, divorce. She'd seen too much to ignore the truth.

Kelsey needed a diversion. Anything would do. She grabbed the Life section of the morning paper and flipped open the front page. Her eyes focused on a headline in the gossip column: Hollywood's Golden Couple To Split.

Talk about vindication. This was what she needed to reaffirm all she believed, what her heart told her was true. So what if Will's kisses could melt an icicle? That didn't mean squat when it came to marriage. She leaned forward to read the article. "I knew it."

"Knew what?" Will asked.

She glanced up to see him carrying Midas into the kitchen and set him down in front of his food bowl. "Another pair of clients are divorcing. The husband has been romantically linked to one of his co-stars, but his publicist denies any other parties are involved."

"That's too bad."

"At least they didn't have any children," Kelsey said. "But they did have a beautiful wedding."

Will shrugged. "You can have the finest wedding ever, but if you don't have a good marriage, the wedding won't count for much except a total waste of time and money."

Her gaze met his. "That wedding was not a waste. It was a lovely celebration. A day for the bride and groom to remember for the rest of their lives."

"A wedding and a marriage are two completely different things. One is an event on a given day. The other is alive. It grows and changes and lasts."

"Only in some cases does it last."

"Do you seriously think any couple wants to remember their wedding once they are no longer married?"

"I..." Kelsey wasn't sure of the answer. She believed the wedding and the marriage were separate entities so the memories would be separate, too. It wouldn't matter if the marriage ended badly. The wedding would still be thought of fondly. "Can I have this article?"

"Go ahead and take it," he said. "It'll be a stellar addition to your divorce book."

She ripped the page out of the paper. "It's a scrapbook, not a divorce book."

"It's sad, that's what it is." He stared at her, an observant gleam in his eyes. "Show business marriages must have a higher rate of divorce than other marriages. Bet that validates your unhappily-ever-after belief. Is that why you became the Wedding Consultant to the Stars?"

"No, I had contacts in the entertainment industry. It just happened."

"You allowed it to happen. With your reputation and skills, you could work anywhere, with anyone. Yet you stay in Tinseltown catering to divorce-happy celebrities. You can't lose."

"You don't know what you're talking about."

"Yes, I do."

She heard his challenge and wanted to respond, but her tongue felt thick in her mouth. Her brain wouldn't function. His words were spinning around in her brain. She couldn't tell her right hand from her left. Nothing made sense. Nothing at all. He was wrong. He had to be wrong. If not...

He was definitely wrong. Kelsey straightened. "Divorce is a fact of life whether you're in Hollywood or Hoboken. The latest statistics show—"

"Marriage isn't about statistics." Will sat next to her, throwing her senses into even further chaos. "It's about a man and a woman who want to spend the rest of their lives going to bed and waking up next to one another."

"Waking up next to the same person every single day of your life?" She shuddered. "Now that's a scary thought."

"Marriage is beyond scary. It's about a love so all-consuming you can't see beyond it. You don't want to see beyond it."

Maybe in his world, not in hers. Love meant misery and pain. All the things she'd seen her parents go through time and time again. Kelsey shrugged. "I can't imagine ever feeling that way about anyone."

"That's only because you haven't met the right person. Once you do, everything falls into place like the pieces of a jigsaw puzzle. You feel complete. It's like magic."

She'd never felt anything remotely like that. An empty space in her heart ached.

"I'm not trying to upset you, Kelsey. I don't want to argue or goad you, either. But you push my buttons like no one else and..." He blew out a puff of air and smiled. "I only want to show you what you're missing out on. What you can't afford to miss out on. Love. It's a wonderful thing."

At that moment she realized how lucky Sara was to have found a man like Will even if they hadn't had long together. Will Addison was one in a million. "I'll take your word on it." Kelsey worked hard to sound as if she couldn't have cared less. But she cared so much it hurt.

"No, you have to find out for yourself."

His gaze held hers for what seemed like forever. "Find out what?" she asked finally.

"How it feels to share your secrets and your dreams and a piece of yourself with one special person."

Let me share them with you. Kelsey's heart lodged in her throat.

"He's out there waiting for you."

No, he's right here.

Will wanted to get to his parents' house A.S.A.P. He cranked up the speed of his wiper to keep his windshield clear of the falling snow and focused on the road. At least the snow wasn't sticking. Dad sounded so excited on the phone. Will couldn't wait to see Mom's progress with the walker for himself.

Part of him felt guilty for leaving. But the other part was relieved to get out of the house. Away from anything and everything related to the upcoming wedding. Away from Kelsey.

Kelsey.

This morning he'd only said what needed to be said. About divorce, marriage and love. She hadn't wanted to hear it, but he owed it to her to tell the truth. Love was a wonderful thing and she needed to know what she was missing. He'd said each and every word for her own good. But it hadn't been for his own good. Will found that out the hard way.

Kelsey's special someone was out there. Will knew in his heart, and he'd never been so envious of a total stranger as he'd been at that moment. As he was right now. One lucky guy was waiting for her. Thinking about it, about *him,* felt weird and wrong and a lot of other things.

But what was he supposed to do about it? That was the million-dollar question, and he needed a final answer.

A memory of Sara came to mind. His sweet Sara on their wedding day. And another on the day she brought Midas home with her for summer break. The memory changed. Only this time it was Kelsey and the first time he'd seen her in her office. And one of Kelsey when she'd picked up Midas for the first time and cuddled him. And yet another of Kelsey kissing him yesterday outside in the snow. Jumbled memories of Sara and Kelsey assaulted him until he could barely see straight let alone drive.

Will turned into his parents' driveway and stopped.

Sweat beaded on his forehead. He tugged on his shirt collar. The only sounds were the engine and the wiper blades. Swish-swish. Swish-swish. Back and forth like the thoughts running through his head. He brushed his hand through his hair.

His memories of Sara were still there. All present and accounted for. Kelsey hadn't eclipsed them, but she had carved her own memories into his mind. And right now he was even more confused than before.

This couldn't be happening.

Standing in Faith's room in front of the movie star's mirror, Kelsey blinked, but nothing changed. She hadn't been dreaming. She had really...

"Whatever it is," Christina said on the opposite end of the phone line. "It can't be that bad."

"It's worse than bad." Kelsey gripped the phone. "I—I'm wearing Faith's wedding gown."

Once the words were out, it didn't seem quite so bad. For about a second. Another look at her reflection and Kelsey bit her lip. Hard.

A loud thud sounded in her ear, and she cringed.

Christina shrieked. "Have you lost your mind?"

"That's one explanation." Kelsey turned to the side to see how the profile of the dress looked. The skirt puddled elegantly at her feet. It would look lovely bustled. On Faith, not her. Kelsey *was* losing her mind. "This must be an ethical violation of the code of conduct for wedding consultants. Not that I've ever read such a thing. But I'm sure one exists—"

"Stop. Right this minute." Christina had never sounded so harried. Must be her pregnancy and all those hormones. Kelsey never should have called her. "Why are you wearing a wedding dress?"

Kelsey wasn't quite sure herself. Blaming it on aliens or ghosts wouldn't cut it. Not with Christina. Kelsey took a deep breath.

"I'm waiting," Christina said.

"Let's see... Will went over to visit his mother. She's been going to rehab to learn to use a walker, and I wanted to put the wreath and veil in Faith's closet so they'd be here when she arrived. And...well...it just sort of happened."

"Putting on a wedding dress does not just happen."

"No, it was hard work to get all the buttons fastened by myself. I now know why brides always need help dressing."

"Kelsey."

The minute the urge hit her to try on the dress, she should have packed her bags and gotten out of town, away from all this wedding nonsense, away from Will. He was the real reason she looked as if she'd stepped out of wedding album from 1910. He'd made her want to feel loved, like a bride. "I uncovered the dress and held up the veil and wreath. It looked so perfect together, I had to see what it would look like on."

"I take it you're not only wearing the dress."

"No." Kelsey adjusted the wreath. "In my defense, can I say the gown and the headpiece look as if they were made for me? And I swear the dress was asking me to put it on."

"A talking wedding dress?" Christina sighed. "Okay, who is this? What have you done with my cousin Kelsey?"

"I didn't mean literally, but it was sort of magical. And I kept smelling roses."

"You caught my bouquet. There were roses in my bouquet."

"That was months ago."

"Maybe there's some leftover magic from the Legend of the Ring."

Magic would be much easier for Kelsey to buy. "You think?"

"I don't know, but it's strange. Even your voice sounds different."

"I feel different, too." It wasn't only the wedding gown and headpiece she wore, either. Her skin glowed, a radiant glow not even the best makeup artists could give her. Her cheeks were flushed, not from the cold, not from heat, not even embarrassment for what she'd done. Her eyes were clear and bright and sparkling. If she could bottle this up, add a catchy name and sell it, she'd be every woman's new best friend.

"What exactly is going on out there?" Concern filled Christina's voice.

"I'm putting together a Valentine's wedding."

"You've planned more weddings than I can count and you've never tried on a wedding dress before. Who is he? There has to be a man involved. Tell me his name."

Christina knew Kelsey too well. "Will. His name is Will Addison. He's the brother of the bride."

"Start at the beginning and tell me everything."

Kelsey imagined Christina plopping down on her bed and sitting cross-legged. Would that be uncomfortable in her position? "You're pregnant and have a lot more to deal with than—"

"Tell me now."

And Kelsey did. She told Christina everything. "I've never met anyone like Will. He's smart, funny, kind, loving, romantic. I'm falling for him, but it will never work because he's still in love with his late wife. He even wears his wedding ring. He believes his wife was perfect and they had the perfect marriage.'' The words tumbled from her lips faster than tears from a flock of bridesmaids during a wedding ceremony. But Kelsey couldn't stop them, didn't want to stop them. It felt so good to get it off her chest and to say the words out loud. "Will believes in one true love and thinks he's already had his chance. He even told me there was someone special waiting for me. Another man, Christina. It's a totally hopeless situation.''

"Look at Richard and me. He wanted to prove the legend wrong, and I wanted nothing to do with a prince. At first it seemed like an impossible situation, but everything worked out in the end.''

"But that's you." Kelsey removed the headpiece. "A happily-ever-after has been waiting for you ever since you were a little girl. Remember how Grandfather Armstrong called you Princess and now you are one. Talk about Fate.''

"Well, he used to call you Tinker Bell.''

"Exactly. A girl who hangs out with a boy who never wants to grow up. Need I say more. I'm not like you. I've never wanted nor tried to find Prince Charming. And now that I have—''

"Will is your Prince Charming?''

Kelsey's mouth parted in surprise. "Did I say that?''

"You did.''

She learned something new every day. Not that it changed anything in this case. In fact, it only made it worse. Maybe when she got back to L.A. she could throw herself a pity party. Send out invitations, order in an obscene amount of chocolate—ice cream, cake, cookies and candy.

"You can't let this chance pass you by," Christina said. "You have to tell him how you feel."

"How can I do that when I'm not even sure myself?"

"Are you in love with him?"

"Love?" Kelsey's voice cracked. "It couldn't be love."

Love was what drove couples to marry. Love was what brought her parents so much misery and heartache. Love was the one thing she wasn't looking for. A lump formed in Kelsey's throat.

But she didn't know how to describe all these new feelings coming to life within her, her heightened senses that made snowflakes come alive, the perpetual smile on her face when she thought about Will.

It couldn't be love.

Could it?

The wind howled, but Will couldn't see anything outside the window except a blanket of white falling from the sky. No moon, no stars, no trees, no mountains. Only snow. Lots and lots of snow. At least Kelsey would be happy. She really seemed to like the white stuff. Of course, there was too much of a good thing. And with Faith and Trent and Hope due in tomorrow for the rehearsal, Will hoped the storm passed by morning.

Wanting to keep busy, he opened a bottle of Merlot and placed it on the coffee table next to a plate of cheese and crackers. With a push of a button on his stereo, the sound of music filled the living room. He added a log to the fireplace and stoked the fire until it blazed.

Above the music, footsteps sounded on the stairs. Kelsey had been upstairs squirreled away hard at work as usual. He hadn't seen her since returning from his parents' house after dinner.

Will turned away from the window and sucked in a breath. Kelsey stood in the doorway, a shy smile on her lips. She wore her hair down, the way he liked best, and the strands gleamed in the lights. Even from this distance, he could smell her perfume.

She took a step toward him. "How did it go?"

He didn't know how a woman could make a pair of black jeans and a white turtleneck look like high fashion, but Kelsey could. "My mom made it across the length of the living room."

Kelsey joined him at the window. "That's wonderful."

He nodded. "She told us to hold our applause until she walked up the stairs."

Kelsey smiled. "That sounds like Starr."

"You think so?"

It was Kelsey's turn to nod. "You sound surprised."

He shrugged. This wasn't something he felt comfortable talking about, but with Kelsey…even the uncomfortable seemed easy. "She seems so different now."

"There will be differences, but I hope you know it could have been a lot worse."

"I know," he admitted. "But it still seems pretty bad to me." He stared at the fireplace. Once his mother had been like those flames. Warm and full of energy. "And…"

Kelsey touched his shoulder. "What?"

"Her risk for another stroke is higher." There, he'd said it, said what had been weighing on him since the first stroke. He took a deep breath. "Another stroke could kill her or completely disable her."

"True, but a million other things could happen and

do the same thing. To your mother, to you.'' Kelsey squeezed his shoulder, then let go. ''You can't worry about what-ifs. That's not good for your mother or for yourself.''

But the risk was real, too real. ''If anything happens to her...''

''Something already did. She had a stroke and survived. Your family has survived, too.''

''No, we haven't. We've been floundering like a ship lost at sea without its captain. We even had to bring in a hired gun to help with the wedding.''

Kelsey arched a brow. ''I've been called a lot of things in my life, but never a hired gun.''

''It was a compliment.''

''Thank you.'' The look in her eyes softened. ''And Will, not every family can handle a wedding on their own. Lots of people use...hired guns.''

''It's not only the wedding.'' Will wished Kelsey would touch him again. Her touch reassured him, made him feel stronger. ''My mom's the one who holds this family together. She always has. Even my dad admits it. Any time there's a problem or something needs to be done or a million other things, my mom's the one to do it or to see that it gets done. And now there's no one.''

A thoughtful smile curved Kelsey's lips. ''There's someone. A co-captain, so to speak.''

Will furrowed his brows. ''Who?''

''You.'' Her smile widened. ''You came to get me. You've done a lot of the work on Faith's wedding. You keep tabs on your mother's progress. Make sure your father isn't getting overwhelmed. You even made travel arrangements for Hope and her family.'' The warmth in

Kelsey's eyes touched Will's heart. "Those are all things your mother would have done."

Her words had such a profound effect on him. He wasn't used to feeling this way, and wasn't sure if he liked it. "So I'm turning into my mom. Just what a guy wants to hear."

Kelsey chuckled. "You're simply stepping up, taking her place for now, like a…pinch runner. I think that's what its called. I'm not much into spectator sports like football."

He laughed. "It's baseball."

"Same difference." She flipped her hair behind her shoulder. "Two teams, a ball, a score, and lots of commercials."

He smiled. "Thanks."

Her forehead wrinkled. "For what?"

"For making me feel better."

All of a sudden he was very aware of his surroundings. The crackling fire. A seductive jazz CD playing on the stereo. The wine, cheese and crackers. The only things missing were candles.

What the hell was he doing?

Will motioned to the coffee table. "I, uh, put out some food in case you were hungry."

Her eyes widened with appreciation. "I'm starving. I skipped lunch and dinner."

"There was a plate for you in the fridge."

"I, um, forgot."

He sat on the couch. "You were really busy today."

"I had a few things I needed to do." She sat on the opposite end of the couch. It was better this way, he told himself. "But I failed to get to the most important thing on my list. Maybe food is what I need to fuel my creativity. I've procrastinated way too long."

"You?" He poured the wine into glasses. "I don't believe it."

"Believe it." She took the glass he offered. "The wedding vows have to be ready by tomorrow. Which leaves tonight. It's just..."

"What?"

"Don't you think it's kind of weird to have someone else write the vows? I mean, if you were getting married, wouldn't you want to write your own?"

"Sara wrote ours."

"Forget I said anything."

"This is no big deal," he said. "Faith's used to reading lines. This won't be any different for her."

"What about Trent?"

"He's a guy." Will grabbed a cracker from the plate. "Do you really think he wants to write his own?"

"I guess not."

The hushed tone of Kelsey's voice told him she was still concerned. She really was...sweet. "If they don't like the vows, they can use whatever the minister brings with him. No big deal. I'll even help."

"I'm making more out of this than I should. How difficult can it be?" Kelsey placed her glass on the table and picked up her notebook and pen. "Dearly Beloved, we are gathered here again and again and again and again and again."

"To unite Faith and—insert groom's name here—in the state of holy matrimony."

Kelsey laughed. "If anyone—four previous grooms excluded—has any reason why these two should not wed..."

He chuckled. "See, this isn't so hard."

She smiled. "No, but we haven't reached the vows yet."

"We have all night for that."

The lights flickered once. The CD stopped playing right on a beautiful high note. Another flicker of the lights, then black except for the glow from the fireplace.

"The storm must have caused a blackout," Will said.

"I hope the electricity is back on soon."

"Out here you never know how long these things will last," Will admitted. "Stay where you are. I'll be right back with candles."

As he walked to the kitchen, Will sighed. Writing wedding vows by candlelight with a woman he wanted to kiss, but couldn't kiss. Not exactly how he imagined spending this evening.

But nothing seemed to ever turn out the way he expected.

Waiting for Will to return, Kelsey settled back against the cushions on the couch and wrapped her hands around her knees. The crackle of the fire, Midas's breathing and the sounds of the storm more than filled the living room. Sitting in near darkness was relaxing, and she relished this moment of peace.

Starting tomorrow, it would be nonstop action until the bride and groom left for their honeymoon. Two days of putting all her planning and organizational skills to the test. Two days until Faith Starr married Trent Jeffreys. Three days until Kelsey headed home to Los Angeles.

Time was running out. She needed to sort through and figure out her feelings for Will. The sooner, the better. She wanted to have things resolved, if only with herself, before she left.

Will returned with two lit candles and placed them on the coffee table. The tapers provided a soft glow—

a romantic glow—of light. Combined with the fire, it was the perfect environment for a kiss. Kelsey's mouth went dry.

No more kisses. She and Will had agreed. It was for the best. Kisses would only interfere with what she needed to do. One kiss and she'd be unable to sort through anything except more kisses.

Will tossed another log on the fire. The muscles of his back strained his shirt. She caught herself staring and looked away. This was about staying warm, nothing else. Kelsey readied her pen. If only her mind would ready itself as easily.

He grabbed several pillows from the couch and tossed them onto the rug in front of the fireplace. "Sit closer to the fire. I want you to stay warm."

Candlelight, a crackling fire, a bearskin rug. Okay, it was an Aubusson, not a bearskin rug. That didn't change the images running through her mind. She kept seeing herself kissing Will except she was wearing Faith's wedding gown and he was in a black tux. Man, he looked handsome in formal attire. Her dry mouth got drier.

"Come on."

With her notebook clutched to her chest, Kelsey joined him on the floor. He tucked a quilted throw around her legs. The thoughtful gesture stirred something deep within her. She placed her notebook on her lap, but held on to the edges. She had to do something to keep from touching him.

Shadows from the fire danced on his face. "Do you need another blanket?"

"I'm fine."

Or at least she would be once her stomach stopped

flipping cartwheels and her heart stopped hammering in her ears.

He grabbed another throw from a chair, anyway, and set it on the floor. "If the electricity stays off, it'll get cold. We may not have any other choice but to sleep down here."

Sleep here together. Not by accident, but by choice. Her pulse quickened.

Who needed a fire or a blanket to keep warm? She didn't. It was getting downright toasty in here.

"What about a poem?" he asked.

"Excuse me?"

"We could use lines of a poem as part of the wedding vows. Something romantic, something lasting. Know any good ones?"

Kelsey closed her eyes. She pictured herself standing next to Will at the altar, about to be married. The image was so clear, so vivid. "'Grow old along with me! The best is yet to be...'" The words flowed from her lips.

"That's beautiful."

"Yes." As was the image in her mind. Perfectly wrong. She wasn't the bride. She was a long way from being a bride. Kelsey opened her eyes and saw Will's smiling face. She gulped. Hard.

"I'm impressed you can recite Browning."

"Don't be impressed. I wasn't reciting anything." Heat flooded her cheeks, and she was thankful the light was from the fireplace and candles. "I read the line in a potpourri catalog and must have memorized it for some reason."

"I love how you come up with this stuff." Will laughed, the rich sound sent shivers of delight down her spine. "Always the cynic, aren't you?"

She didn't want to be a cynic. Not anymore. Something was happening to her. Something Kelsey didn't understand. Tears stung her eyes, and she blinked them away.

"What if we rewrite some of the traditional vows?"

What if they forgot the entire thing? She swallowed around the lump. "You mean, 'I, Faith, take you Trent, to be my husband. To have and to hold, from this day forward...yadda, yadda, yadda."

"Yadda, yadda, yadda?"

Kelsey concentrated on the vows. It had always been easy to lose herself in work. Maybe too easy, she realized. "'For better or for worse, in sickness and in health, for richer, for poorer.'"

"Cherish, promise, pledge, vow."

"Honor, respect, that sort of stuff."

Will grinned. "All the stuff that gives you the willies?"

Forcing a smile, she nodded. "Do you want to start?"

"I'd be honored." He scooted closer to her. Too close for her own good. The space in front of the fireplace wasn't large, but it was big enough for him to keep his distance. "I, Trent, take you, Faith, to be my wife."

"I could have come up with that." Kelsey wrote down the words. "Wait a minute, I already did."

He chuckled. "I'm just warming up. It's your turn now."

She glanced up from her notebook. "My turn?"

"We're in this together. I come up with a line, then you come up with one."

"Fair enough." Waiting for inspiration to strike, Kelsey tapped her pen on the notebook. She glanced over at Will. "Today in front of our family and friends, I pledge my love and my fidelity."

"That's a good one."

His compliment made her feel all tingly inside. She smiled. "Thank you."

"I promise to be your husband, your lover and your friend."

His smile, so sincere and open, made Kelsey feel as if he were making those promises to her. She wanted him to be making those promises to her. Just as she wanted to make the same promises to him. Warmth pooled low in her belly and started to spread. "I vow to be your faithful partner and to stay by your side in good times and in bad."

"I will honor you, respect you, cherish you."

The look in his eyes took her breath away. Breathe, she reminded herself, but the last thing she needed at the moment was air. She needed Will.

He moved closer, his gaze never leaving hers. "I will put you and our family first and never let an argument go beyond sunset."

Happily ever after.

She could taste it. She could feel it. She wanted it. Never mind that it went against everything she'd believed in for most of her life. She couldn't help herself. Not when she could suddenly picture a future with a man by her side, and that man was Will Addison. An image so appealing it made her heart sing. Something so wonderful had to be right.

And that's when it hit her.

She loved Will Addison.

Kelsey Armstrong Waters loved William Addison IV.

Loved him with her heart and her soul. "I promise to listen to you, to laugh with you, to love you."

A featherlight brush of Will's hand made her nerve endings dance. His smile softened and he rested his hand on hers. "And when our time on this world does end, our love here will continue on for eternity."

Eternity. Kelsey's heart sunk to her feet. She pulled her hand away and picked up the pen that had slipped from her fingers. Yes, she loved Will, but his belief in one true love, in a love so all-consuming to last through eternity, would keep him from ever loving her.

He'd already found his one true love.

And it wasn't her.

Chapter Ten

February 13

So much for happily ever after.

Only seventeen minutes until the rehearsal was scheduled to begin, and there had been no word from Faith or Trent. Were they or weren't they going to show?

Bill and Starr sat in the living room holding hands and quietly talking with the minister. Neither looked overly concerned.

Hope, the matron of honor, looked more tired than anxious. At the moment she was in the kitchen feeding a snack to her children. She was everything Will had described and more. Her stylishly short hair, a cap of dark brown curls, accented her natural beauty and didn't need lots of work. With a peaches-and-cream complexion to die for and lush dark lashes, she needed no makeup. Good thing since it seemed Hope had little

time for herself with three little ones hanging all over
her. She kept popping into the living room to see what
was going on until a ''Mommy'' cry would pull her
back into the kitchen.

But Will was another story. As he stood at a window
staring out at the driveway, Kelsey caught a glimpse of
his profile. His jaw was clenched, his features tight. Her
heart went out to him. She wanted to kiss him and hold
him and make everything better. But that was the last
thing she could do. She glanced at her watch again.

Don't let your family down, Faith.

Don't let me down.

Kelsey was the first to admit she'd had doubts about
Faith showing up, but Kelsey wanted to be proven
wrong. This wasn't the wedding of Starr's dreams, it
was the wedding of Kelsey's dreams. She never thought
it would happen, wasn't quite sure how or when it happened, but it had. Somewhere between planning Faith's
wedding, Kelsey had planned her own.

And she wasn't going to let Faith screw it up. Forget
about having cold feet, second thoughts, jitters. It was
too late for that.

Kelsey wanted to see Faith walk down the staircase
wearing the wedding dress and the vintage headpiece.
She wanted to hear Faith recite the wedding vows and
say, ''I do.'' She wanted to know Faith and Trent would
find eternal love and happiness in each other's arms.

Nothing less would do.

''Here she comes.'' Relief sounded in his voice and
sent a wave of it washing over Kelsey. Thank you, she
muttered.

As Will hurried to the front door, Kelsey followed
him. She glanced at her watch. Fifteen minutes to spare.
At least Faith, Trent and the best man, who happened

to be the groom's brother, weren't late. That had to be a good sign.

The door swung open. Clad in a purple cape and matching hat, Faith entered with a flourish. She greeted Will with a hug, then turned to Kelsey. "You're looking lovely. The mountain air agrees with you."

Kelsey smiled. "Thanks."

Faith removed her cape and hat and hung them on the coat tree. She brushed her fingers through her long, wavy locks of hair that made women everywhere envious. No hair extensions for Faith Starr. "Where are Mom and Dad?"

"In the living room." Will looked out the front door. "Are Trent and his brother at the inn?"

Faith took Will's hand. "Let's go in the living room."

He exchanged a confused look with Kelsey. All she could do was shrug. Something was going on, but Faith didn't seem overly concerned or upset. She might be an award-winning actress, but no one was that good when it came to their own lives. Maybe Trent was running late.

"Hello, everyone." Faith made her way to Starr and gave her a kiss on the cheek. "You look wonderful, Mom."

"Where's Trent?" Starr asked.

"He's..." Faith wet her full lips, lips one studio executive suggested she insure with Lloyd's of London for seven figures. "He's not coming."

Kelsey never expected the groom to be a no-show. Her heart plummeted to her feet. She sank into the nearest chair she could find as a mix of emotion churned inside her. Anger, sadness, frustration, confusion. She'd always known this was a possibility, but she'd hoped, really hoped.

Starr's mouth gaped open. "Not c-c-coming?"

Wrinkles of concern lined Bill's forehead. "The wedding's tomorrow."

Faith took a deep breath. "There isn't going to be a wedding."

Kelsey glanced at Will, who stared at her speechless. For the first time in a long time, saying I-told-you-so would give her zero pleasure. Tears welled in her eyes.

"What happened?" Starr asked.

"W-we..." Faith's voice faltered.

"You made it." Hope entered the living room, a dish towel in her hands. She dabbed the towel at a wet spot on the front of her heather-gray jumper. The arms and shoulders of her white turtleneck were smudged with chocolate. "Where's Trent?"

The tears glistening in Faith's eyes ran down her cheeks like the spring thaw of the Sierra snowpack.

Hope ran to her sister's side. "What did I say?"

Will wrapped his arms around Faith. "There isn't going to be a wedding."

Hope started to cry as did Starr. Kelsey watched the exchange of support, hugs, tears with amazement. Yes, she was the outsider and didn't mean to be unfeeling, but wasn't anyone else interested in knowing why the wedding had been called off?

"What happened with Trent?" Starr asked, to Kelsey's gratitude.

"I found out he wasn't...we weren't." Faith blinked. "He wasn't the one."

"Come here, sweetheart." Bill hugged her. "It's better to cancel before the wedding, than after. Marriage is too big a step to rush into. You don't want to make a mistake.''

"I don't." Faith stared at Starr. "I'm sorry, Mom. I know how much you wanted me to marry Trent, but I…couldn't.''

"It's okay, honey." Starr's sincerity made Kelsey want to cry. The love between mother and daughter was so strong you could almost touch it. "The most important thing is your happiness.''

"That's right. There's someone out there for you." Hope smiled. "You'll find 'the one,' get married and live happily ever after.''

Bill smoothed Faith's hair. "Your true love is out there. Don't give up.''

"Hope and I found ours early," Will added. "You've always been a late bloomer. That's why it's taking you longer.''

Found ours. Kelsey stared at the band of gold on Will's finger. Her heart lodged in her throat.

Faith nodded, but the sadness in her eyes made Kelsey feel sorry for her. Sorry for one of the most beautiful, talented and sought-after stars in Hollywood. More sorry than Kelsey felt for herself at the moment. A bad day was one thing, but this…

She wanted to shake some sense into the Addisons. Couldn't they see they weren't helping? Putting pressure on Faith by telling her Mr. Right was out there waiting for her wasn't what she needed.

No wonder Faith had such a problem getting to the "I do." She had her entire family, all the Addison ancestors and their history of marrying their "one true love," to live up to. The Addisons' unrealistic expectations of love and marriage were the problem, not Faith. She was only trying not to disappoint her family.

As her family continued to comfort Faith, Kelsey's anger rose. At the Addisons, at herself. Kelsey's parents' lack of expectation of love and marriage had as negative an effect on her as Faith's family's unrealistic expectation about love and marriage did on her.

Kelsey couldn't take it any longer. She stood. "Excuse me." All eyes focused on her.

"What is it, Kelsey?" Will asked.

The words were on the tip of her tongue. Words that needed to be said to put an end to this nonsense. But she wasn't a family member; she wasn't even a family friend. She was the wedding consultant. "I need to make a few phone calls about tomorrow's…anniversary party."

Staring at her empty, but open suitcase, Kelsey sat on her bed with a new To Do list in front of her. She should start packing, but she still had a job to do. The anniversary party backup plan was officially in effect. The beautiful wedding she and Will had planned and worked so hard to make a reality was history.

Disappointment rocketed through her. She'd never felt this way when Faith had canceled her other weddings, or any other bride for that matter. But this wedding had been different. Kelsey had never put so much into designing a wedding before. Her heart and soul had gone into each and every detail.

But it went deeper than that. Much deeper.

A knock sounded on her door. "Come in," she said. Will entered. "How's it going?"

She didn't want to tell him that having options—ones he said were unnecessary—were making the transition from wedding to anniversary party easy. She didn't want to tell him how much working with him these past two weeks had meant to her. She didn't want to tell him about the mix of emotions racing through her right now. "Okay."

He noticed her suitcase. "Going somewhere?"

"I thought I might move over to the inn now that the wedding is off."

"Why?"

"The last thing your family needs is to have me hanging around. They need privacy, and it'll be easier for me to oversee the party preparations from there." Before giving him a chance to change her mind, she continued. "How is Faith doing?"

"Better." The tightness around his mouth eased. "She'll be okay. There's someone out there for her—"

"Stop it."

"Stop what?"

"Faith doesn't need to hear about finding her one true love right now. She just broke up with her fiancé and canceled yet another wedding. Give her some time to catch her breath, not get all pumped up to find Mr. Right."

"There's nothing wrong with telling her—"

"Yes, there is." Kelsey cut Will off. The words she'd wanted to say earlier had to be said. "If you would leave Faith alone and stop putting so much pressure on her to find 'the one,' she would have been married with a couple of kids by now. Can't you see what you and your family are doing to her?"

Will frowned. "We're not doing anything to her."

"You're influencing how she views love and marriage."

"We're trying to help her."

"The best way to help is to let her figure that out on her own. It's her life, not yours or your family's."

Kelsey's words echoed in her own mind. Realization hit her with the force of a 7.8 earthquake. She had allowed her parents to influence the way she viewed love and marriage as much as Faith had. Different views, but similar outcomes.

And it was time for Kelsey to change that.

She was resisting love for all the wrong reasons. Her feelings were new. Of course, there would be uncertainty and doubts. But that didn't mean those feelings were wrong. There weren't any guarantees in life, why would she assume there would be with love? And she deserved a happy ending as much as the next person.

"We never meant…"

"I know that, and I'm sure Faith knows that, too." Kelsey smiled. "Faith will find someone to love and marry and live happily ever after with, but let her do it on her own terms without any pressure from any of you."

He did a double take. "Did I hear you correctly?"

Kelsey nodded. Time to put up or shut up. At this point, she had nothing to lose. "What would you say if…" Her courage faltered.

"What?"

Kelsey had to do this. Now. Whatever Will's reaction, she had to take the chance or live with the regret. "Would you come with me to San Montico?"

"San Montico?"

"I'd like to see my cousin, and I thought it might be nice if you…we…went together. We could see how we get along away from all this wedding planning."

"We don't need to get away to know we get along."

Her heart filled with hope. "It might be fun."

Will paused. Her heart thudded so loudly she wondered if he could hear it. "If I said yes and we went

away together, you know that's all I could give you.
Once we got back, it would be over. Is that enough for
you?''

"No." Her quick answer surprised Kelsey as much
as Will. "Before you and your family presented such a
strong case for true love and happily ever after I may
have considered it, but now…" She stared into his eyes.
"Don't you even want to try?"

"There's nothing to try."

Kelsey felt as if she'd been slapped in the face.
"Guess I asked for that one."

"I didn't mean—"

"Yes, you did." As he brushed his hand through his
hair, the gold band on his finger sparkled, reflecting the
light from the lamp. He still wasn't over Sara. Nothing
Kelsey could do or say was going to change that.
"It…okay."

Okay that he didn't need her. Okay that he didn't
want her. Okay that he didn't love her.

This love stuff really hurt. She felt as if she'd just
found her heart only to lose it in the same instant. No
guarantees, she reminded herself. Too bad that didn't
make her feel any better, hurt any less.

"I never meant to hurt you," he said, his eyes full
of regret. "I do care about you."

Care, not love. She wouldn't settle for anything less
than the whole enchilada. Will couldn't give that to her.
Someday, after a few years of therapy, she might find
someone who could.

"Say something," he said. "Please."

"You're a hypocrite."

"Excuse me?"

"You wax on about how important love is for everyone but yourself. The last thing you want is to find love

again and have a happily-ever-after. You're no different than me except I was at least honest about my feelings.''

He stared at her. ''I tried after Sara died, but you can't replace perfection.''

''You told me yourself no one is perfect.''

''That's different.''

''Why? Because it's safer to view the past with rose-colored glasses?''

''Don't do this.''

''Do what? Tell the truth?''

''We've had fun. Can't we leave it at that?''

''I guess we're going to have to, aren't we?''

''I don't want you to hate me.''

''I don't hate you, I...'' Kelsey almost laughed when she realized she was about to tell him she loved him. Talk about bad timing. ''I want to thank you. You and your family opened up my mind and my heart to everything I was missing out on before.''

''Missing?''

''Happily-ever-after and all that stuff.''

His eyes widened. ''Does that include marriage?''

''Only time will tell. Right now I'm taking tiny baby steps.'' And even those felt like Sasquatch-size strides at the moment. ''Though I will admit, I don't and won't ever buy into the one love of a lifetime you Addisons prescribe to.''

Thank goodness, Kelsey realized. Otherwise she'd be spending the rest of her life alone since she was sure Will could be hers.

He stared at her, an unreadable expression on his face.

''But I can easily live with true love.'' She flipped

her hair behind her shoulder and looked him square in the eyes. "I just wonder how you can live without it."

Don't walk away from her, a voice cried out in Will's head as he left Kelsey's room. But he ignored it. Ignored the way her words had rocked his world. Ignored how walking out of her room felt like one of the stupidest things he'd ever done.

But he had no choice.

"It would never work," he said out loud as he entered the kitchen. "I already had my chance."

"Talking to yourself, big brother?" The rims of Faith's eyes were red from crying, but at least the tears no longer flowed. "It must be serious."

"It's nothing."

Faith raised an arched brow. "Then why do you look as if you've lost your best friend?"

Because I have. The thought slammed into him with the force of a three-hundred-pound offensive lineman. What was he thinking? Kelsey wasn't his best friend. He hardly knew her. The last thing he felt was indifference, but he shrugged, anyway.

Faith poured him a cup of coffee. "This doesn't have anything to do with Kelsey, does it?"

"Why would you think that?"

"I noticed the glances the two of you exchanged," Faith admitted. "What's going on?"

"Nothing."

"Your choice or hers?"

"Mine."

"How do you feel about her?"

The emotions nearly overwhelmed him. He didn't, couldn't, say anything.

"You've got it bad." Faith tsked. "Why aren't you doing something about it?"

He hesitated. "Sara."

Faith pursed her lips. "Don't sacrifice a second chance at love for a memory."

"Sara's more than a memory." He looked away. "She was my life."

"I know how much you loved Sara. I loved her, too," Faith admitted. "But none of us know what would have happened had she lived."

"What do you mean?"

"Your marriage."

"My marriage was...fine." He couldn't quite bring himself to say perfect.

"Of course it was. But with all your traveling, Sara's graduate school. Who knows what might have happened?"

"Have you been talking to Mom about this?"

"No."

"I loved Sara. I'll always love her."

"But she's gone, Will." Faith squeezed his shoulder. "Sara wouldn't want you to spend the rest of your life alone."

"I'm not alone."

"You are alone," Faith said. "It's time you took off the blinders and realized it yourself. Go ahead and say goodbye to Kelsey, but at least acknowledge what you're losing."

With that, Faith left the room. Always the drama princess, but her flare had paved her way to stardom. But in this instance she couldn't be more wrong.

Will put on his jacket and gloves. He needed to get out of here. Away from everyone and everything for a few minutes.

The cold stung his lungs, but he wasn't about to turn back. He needed to get his head on straight. He hiked up a path to a viewpoint overlooking the lake. A squirrel chattered overhead in a nearby tree.

Sara used to love it here. Memories of her and their time together filled his mind. Life with her had been so perfect. And their marriage…a never-ending honeymoon.

A honeymoon.

His mother's letter came back to him. *An extended honeymoon.* That's what she'd called it; that's exactly what it had been. Not only for the two years of marriage, but also the four years before when they'd attended different colleges.

Damn. His mother was right. Faith, too.

Will brushed his hand through his hair. He and Sara loved each other, lived for each other, but their marriage hadn't been real. They never had to make any of the day-in-and-out compromises necessary for a marriage to succeed.

Hell, what he and Kelsey shared planning Faith's wedding was more of a marriage with compromise and give-and-take than what he and Sara had ever shared.

It had been so easy to cling to the fantasy. To cling to the image of one love of a lifetime. To cling to the notion of what his and Sara's future would have been.

Because it was safe and kept his heart from having to love and lose again.

Loving meant losing. Hurting. Being left behind.

Losing Sara had tilted his world on its axis and spun it around in the opposite direction. He wasn't sure he could survive it again. And that scared him.

But something scared him more. He hadn't kept his heart safe. If he wasn't careful, he was going to lose again. And it would be his fault. Will turned around and headed back to the house.

The safety net surrounding his heart was gone. His mother's stroke had put a tear into it. But Kelsey was the one who had demolished it.

He had to act fast. He had to show Kelsey he'd made a mistake. He needed her to be a part of his life.

Today, tomorrow, always.

Chapter Eleven

Gazing out the bedroom window, Kelsey caught sight of the sun peeking out from a cloud. No more flakes fell from the sky, but snow covered every inch on the ground, all the tree branches and the roof of a gazebo. But rather than a winter wonderland, the landscape seemed gray and foreboding.

Arctic air seeped through the pane-glass window. Kelsey shivered. Too bad the cold wasn't the only thing giving her the chills. But she didn't want to think about that right now.

Time to pack. It was the only thing Kelsey could think to do, next to walking out and leaving everything behind. She emptied her clothes from the dresser and piled them on the bed. If she hadn't been so organized with a backup plan ready to go, she'd have more phone calls to make, more changes to implement. Her mind wouldn't be so focused on Will; her heart wouldn't feel so empty.

But she had been organized, and it wouldn't take her

fifteen minutes to take the storybook wedding she'd
planned for Faith and Trent and turn it into an anniversary party for Starr and Bill. Kelsey folded her red cashmere sweater. She put all her energy into the task and
pretended the emotions churning inside her weren't so
raw, so painful.

Will's rejection stung. Like a wound to her heart no
amount of medical technology could fix. It wasn't even
worth a second opinion. Over time, the hurt would heal.
The memories would fade. His hold on her heart would
disappear.

She *would* survive. She had survived the breakup of
her parents. She would survive a broken heart. Kelsey
had a good life. She had family and friends and a wonderful career. Just because Will didn't want her didn't
mean her life was over. Just the opposite. Her life was
only beginning.

Kelsey went to place her sweater in her suitcase, but
found Midas inside sprawled on his back. She rubbed
his belly, then gave him a gentle push. "Sorry, handsome. You can't sleep here."

The cat merely stretched, taking up more room.

"You are such a sweetie." She scratched his neck.
*Maybe a pet was what she needed. Someone she could
simply love with no baggage to worry about. Someone
who would love her back.* "I wish I could bring you
home with me, but your daddy wouldn't let me."

Daddy.

An image of Will with children appeared in her mind.
Kelsey closed her eyes. She could picture them and feel
them and hear them. Will's children. Her children. Their
children.

The depth of the emotion swelling inside her took
Kelsey's breath away. Her heart pounded fiercely. Tears

stung her eyes. She gathered Midas into her arms and buried her face against his fur.

What was happening to her? A broken heart was one thing, but this? Talk about a one-hundred-and-eighty-degree shift in what she thought she wanted out of life. A pet was one thing, but children, too? It was as if her dormant biological clock was trying to make up for lost time, and Kelsey was torn. Part of her didn't want to waste a single minute, yet the other part wanted to crawl into the closet and lock herself away from the world.

She rubbed her cheek against Midas. His jackhammer purr brought a welcome smile to her lips. "I'm going to miss you, handsome."

"What about me?" At the sound of Will's voice, Kelsey looked up. He stood in the doorway to her room. "Are you going to miss me as much as you'll miss my cat?"

"I…" She tightened her hold on Midas and cuddled him closer. No matter what pain she was feeling, she'd given it her all. Will was the one who wasn't willing to take a chance. She could walk away with no regrets. "I don't think so."

Will raised a brow. "Oh, really?"

Kelsey nodded. It surprised her to realize how much she meant it. Will was the one who was afraid to love again. "Midas goes after what he wants. He isn't afraid to ask for love. You've got to respect that in a man."

"Midas is a cat."

"A male cat." She placed Midas on the bed. "That's close enough for me."

"We need to talk."

"Talk?" Talking to Will again wasn't something she could handle right now. Her frazzled emotions could only take so much. She folded a pair of jeans and placed them in her suitcase. "There's nothing to talk about."

"There's plenty to discuss."

"You made your feelings—or rather your lack of feelings—clear. It's best if we leave it that way." She folded a white blouse. "If you're worried about me, don't be. I might have wished for a different ending, but I'm not about to sit around mourning the loss of an unrequited love."

"What are you going to do?"

"Go find him."

"Find who?"

"Mr. Right." Kelsey dropped the neatly folded shirt back on the bed. "Somewhere in the world is a man who'll want the love I have to give. All I have to do is find him."

"What if he finds you?"

The look in Will's eyes made Kelsey swallow hard. "That'll make my job easier."

"You never take the easy way out. Not the way I do."

She glanced up at him. "When have you—"

"Every chance I've gotten." His eyes darkened. "My entire life things have been handed to me. This house. My job. Even Sara. Remember when you asked me about planning my wedding?"

Kelsey nodded.

"Not only did I not help plan the wedding, I wasn't even the one who proposed. Sara made it easy for me. She had our entire life mapped out from the time we met. She made sure we stayed together and nothing went wrong. I didn't have to do anything except sit back and enjoy the ride. It was so easy with her." He took a step toward Kelsey. "You aren't easy."

"Never claimed to be."

"You've never claimed to be anything other than what you are. I respect that about you. Me, on the other hand, I've been hiding. Hiding from the truth, hiding from my fears."

She stepped back. "You don't have to tell me this."

"Yes, I do." He took a deep breath. "I want another chance."

Her pulse was racing so fast, she thought her veins might explode. She took a calming breath. And another. "I can't do this."

"Yes, you can." He stared into her eyes, and she felt her resolve start to melt. Kelsey looked away. "We've both changed," he said.

"But not enough." She picked up a turtleneck and folded it. "Not enough for it to make a difference."

"Give me the chance. Please."

The sincerity of his plea touched her soul. Her heart pounded, but something—no, someone—held her back—Sara. "I won't compete with a ghost. I can't…"

"You won't have to," he said. "I loved Sara and she'll always hold a special place in my heart. But I've been hiding behind that love and this ring." He removed the gold band from his finger and held it up. "I never realized it until I met you.

"I used Sara and our marriage to keep me safe, keep my heart safe. After she died, I was afraid. Afraid of loving and losing again. When you asked me if I dated, I didn't tell you the only women I dated were those who reminded me of Sara. I wanted to replace her, replace what we shared. I thought if I could, things would be okay. That I could love and pretend I hadn't lost everything when she died. But I failed miserably. You can't replace someone, and you sure can't find perfection. Sara wasn't perfect. Our marriage wasn't perfect, but I couldn't see that. I didn't want to see it." He placed his wedding ring in his pocket. "Until you."

A lump formed in Kelsey's throat. Her knees felt wobbly. She sat on the bed and Midas snuggled against her thigh.

Will walked toward her. "Sara's death. My mother's stroke. I can pretend all I want, but it doesn't change the fact. You can't control what happens."

"Love holds no guarantees."

"It doesn't. No matter how hard you try, you can still lose." He stared into Kelsey's eyes. "I don't want to lose you. I can't lose you." Will reached out and caught her hand in his. "I know we haven't known each other long, but I love you. I tried to fight it. I tried to pretend I didn't. But I do. I love you."

Kelsey sat speechless. She never expected to hear those words from Will's lips. She never expected three little words to have such an impact on her. Yet it still wasn't enough. "Why? Why do you love me?"

The edges of his mouth curled up. "I love the way your eyes light up when something pleases you and how your eyebrows knot together when something doesn't. I love the way you make coffee and the lipstick marks you leave on the mug. I love how you can be cynical, yet wildly romantic about weddings at the same time. Want me to go on?"

She nodded.

He chuckled. "I love that you aren't afraid to speak your mind, give an opinion or tell me I'm wrong even when I'm right. I love how staring into your eyes makes me forget everything, including my own name. I love you, Kelsey. More than I ever thought possible. Enough?"

"For now." She blinked back tears. "Oh, Will. I love you, too."

"Why?" He grinned. "You had me spell it out. Fair is fair."

She laughed. "Let's see...I love how you hand feed Midas his food when you think no one is looking. I love your optimism, your idealism and your kisses. I love your dedication and loyalty to your family and how it has made me want to have a family of my own. Something I thought I never wanted, but deep down truly did. My whole life I felt like something was missing, and I found it when I met you. Enough?"

"For now." He kissed each of her fingertips and tingles shot up her arm. "Say you'll give me a chance. I'll do whatever it takes. Marry me, don't marry me. I don't care as long as we can be together forever."

Kelsey's heart swelled with joy. "I like the sound of forever."

"Me, too."

"You might not want to get used to having a bare ring finger."

"Excuse me?"

"Well, your family has a pretty good record when it comes to marriage, so that might make up for my parents. And since your parents can't adopt me, this is probably my only chance to become a member of your family. Kelsey Armstrong Waters Addison has a nice ring to it. I'm sure I could think of other reasons if you give me a few minutes."

"I thought you were only taking baby steps right now."

"I feel lucky," she admitted. "I did catch the bouquet at my cousin Christina's wedding so I'm the next to wed. And since you happen to be a firm believer in tradition…''

"Does this mean you'd…would you…?'' He brushed his hand through his hair. "Who am I kidding? We've never even been on a date.''

"True, but we've planned a wedding together. That has to count for at least three to six months of dating.''

"I'd say a year.''

"I've never dated anyone for a year so I'll have to take your word for it.'' She grinned. "So…?''

"This is insane.''

"I'm new at this sort of thing, but isn't love normally insane?''

"In this case, yes.'' He raised her right hand and kissed the top of it. "Kelsey Armstrong Waters, would you marry me?''

She stared at him. "I only plan for this to happen once, and I want everything to be perfect. Well, as perfect as we can get it. Do you think you could get down on one knee and try again?''

He smiled. "Anything else?''

"I don't suppose you have a carriage pulled by white horses outside and a dozen red roses?''

"Sorry. We can wait.''

"No, we can't.'' She shifted on the bed, making herself comfortable. Midas simply scooted back up beside her. "I'm ready now.''

Will kneeled and took her hand in his. "Marry me, Kelsey. Be my wife and let me be your husband.''

The words were music to her ears, candy to her mouth. She let them sink in. Closing her eyes, she sighed.

"Kelsey? Are you okay?''

"I'm savoring the moment.''

"Don't forget about the guy on his knee waiting for an answer."

She opened her eyes. "I'm done savoring."

"And?"

"Yes." She smiled. "I'll marry you."

He rose, pulled her into her arms and kissed her. "What do you say we get married tomorrow?"

She was dizzy from his proposal, from his kiss. "Tomorrow? Isn't that a little fast?"

"I doubt we could plan a wedding any more perfect for us."

That was the truth. And she might be able to borrow Faith's dress. It fit, after all. The familiar scent of roses filled the room. "Do you smell that?"

"What?"

"It's nothing," she said. Nothing but a sign marrying Will was the right thing to do. Not that she needed anything except her heart to tell her what to do. "A Valentine's wedding would be romantic."

"I can think of something even more romantic."

"What's that?"

"A Valentine's honeymoon."

"What about a happily-ever-after ending?"

He kissed her. "That's a given."

"Promise?"

"I promise."

Epilogue

February 14, Valentine's Day

Today was her wedding day.

Kelsey stood at the top of the staircase, her father at her side. The mahogany banister was decorated with a garland of flowers, greenery and twinkling white lights. It was just as romantic as she'd imagined it would be the first time she stepped into Will's—soon-to-be their—house. The sweet scent of the roses on the garland and in her bouquet tickled her nose, and she smiled.

It was almost time.

The din of the wedding guests along with the music from the string quartet rose from the living room. She wanted to pinch herself to make sure this wasn't a dream, but she didn't want to snag the lace fabric of her gown. Faith had graciously offered the use of her wedding dress last night. Kelsey had accepted without a moment's hesitation, brushing aside any concerns about whether alterations would be needed. As far as she was concerned, no one except Christina and, one day soon, Will, would ever know she'd tried on the dress before.

Christina.

She was the only person missing. She'd wanted to come, but travelling such a long way with morning sickness would have been too much for her. Kelsey knew that her cousin would be with her in spirit, accompanying her every step of the way down the aisle.

There's something about the magical power of love.

That's what Christina had told her once. Kelsey had rolled her eyes then. She was a believer now. Perhaps a sprinkle of magic had travelled all the way from San Montico. How else could she explain everything that had happened these past two weeks? That was about to happen...

Her maid of honor, Faith, and her matron of honor, Hope, descended the staircase to the strains of "Canon in D." The song wasn't the most original when it came to processional music, but Kelsey didn't care. It had always been one of her favorites. That's all that mattered today. *She* was the bride.

Faith and Hope turned the corner. A few moments later, a new song began—Mozart's "Romance from String Quartet." Each note was like a kiss, rising up to greet Kelsey.

This is it.

"Even though you'll be a married woman, you'll always be my little girl." Her father, Charles Waters, kissed her cheek. "Are you ready, sweetheart?"

Kelsey smiled, delighted her brother and her parents

had dropped everything and flown to Nevada for the impromptu wedding. "I'm ready."

Each step brought her closer to her groom, to her new life, and she couldn't wait. She and her father rounded the corner. At the front of the living room in front of the fireplace stood the minister, her brother, Cade, and Will.

Will.

She should have known he would look great in a tuxedo. He would look great in anything. Or nothing. She'd know tonight. Kelsey grinned.

Will's wide smile softened. She felt so cherished, so loved. She never wanted this moment to end. Everything she'd never realized she'd wanted—*needed* was standing right in front of her.

As she made her way down the makeshift aisle, his gaze never left hers. Forty-six other people in the living room turned wedding chapel, but she barely noticed their presence.

The love shining in Will's eyes took Kelsey's breath away. Warmth, joy, euphoria filled her heart and her soul. The depth of the emotions, the intensity of the feelings overwhelmed her. And she loved it. This was what life was all about.

She heard her father say "Her mother and I," but Kelsey hadn't heard the minister ask his question.

Her father kissed her cheek and placed her hand in Will's. Will gave her a gentle squeeze. His gaze held hers. She didn't want to look away. Ever. She saw her future in his eyes. A future full of love, laughter, family. A future with a happily-ever-after ending.

He couldn't take his eyes off her.

Will had never seen a more stunning bride in his life.

It wasn't only the breathtaking vintage dress, headpiece and veil Kelsey wore, either. She glowed, a radiant light that poured through her smile, her eyes, everything. It didn't get much better than this. He grinned.

"Kelsey and Will have written wedding vows of their own," the minister announced to the friends and family gathered in the living room. "Kelsey."

She stared into Will's eyes. "I, Kelsey Armstrong Waters, take you, William Drake Addison, to be my husband. Today in front of our family and friends, I pledge my love and fidelity."

This wonderful, intelligent woman was going to be *his* wife. Awe mixed with pride. He was the luckiest guy in the world.

Her eyes glimmered as she continued on with the vows. Suddenly, she faltered, her voice clogging with emotion. "...and s-s-stay by your side in good times and in bad."

A single tear ran down her cheek, and a lump formed in Will's throat. She was so beautiful. He caressed her cheek, brushing the happy tear away.

She smiled. "I—I promise to listen to you, to laugh with you, to love you..."

Only two nights ago, she'd said those same words right here in his living room. So much, no everything had changed since then. And he couldn't be happier.

She looked up, her eyes brimming with tears. "...all the days of my life."

It was his turn. He didn't know how he remembered the words and managed to say them without making a total fool of himself, but he drew strength from Kelsey. From her presence. From her smile. Each word meant so much to him, and Kelsey's tears showed him she felt the same way.

The time arrived for the ring exchange. Kelsey held the band of gold with her fingertips. "With this ring I thee wed."

Her hand trembled as she slid the ring onto his finger. The look of pure joy in her eyes touched his soul, and he felt whole. One-hundred-percent complete.

Time to pull himself together or he was never going to get the matching gold band on her finger. He swallowed. Hard. "With this ring, I thee wed."

With Will at her side, Kelsey watched the guests eat, drink, dance and be merry. The same things guests do at any reception, but this one was different because it was *her* wedding. Those were her guests. And Will was her husband.

Husband.

She really liked the sound of that.

The clinking of silverware against glass had Will leaning over to kiss her. They'd kissed so many times since the wedding ceremony, she'd lost count. Now to keep it up tomorrow and the next day and the next.

"I could get used to doing this," he said.

She grinned. "I'm counting on it."

"The only thing left on your schedule is the bouquet and garter toss," Will whispered. "What do you say we do those and get out of here?"

"That's the best offer I've had all night."

As the single women gathered on the dance floor, Kelsey noticed, Faith hadn't joined them, so she had Cade bring her forward. Much to Faith's dismay, Kelsey realized. Oh, well. What were the odds?

With Will at her side, she turned around and tossed the bouquet over her shoulder. The crowd gasped. Kelsey turned to see who the lucky woman was. What she saw was a very red-faced, angry Faith, holding the bouquet in front of her as if it were a dirty, smelly diaper.

"You know what this means, don't you?" Kelsey smiled to Will. "Faith will be the next one to get married."

He laced his fingers with Kelsey's, his brand-new shiny band of gold brushing her finger. Poor Faith, she didn't stand a chance. Kelsey chuckled.

Will kissed her. Short, but oh-so-sweet. "Don't get your hopes up, my love."

My love. She sighed. "I have a feeling this is out of Faith's hands now."

"I hate to be the one to say it, but I've come to the conclusion that my youngest sister will never get married."

"Never say never." Kelsey grinned. "Trust me on this one, okay?"

* * * * *

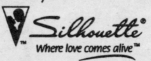

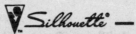

Feel like a star with Silhouette.

We will fly you and a guest to New York City for an exciting weekend stay at a glamorous 5-star hotel. Experience a refreshing day at one of New York's trendiest spas and have your photo taken by a professional. Plus, receive $1,000 U.S. spending money!

Flowers...long walks...dinner for two... how does Silhouette Books make romance come alive for you?

Send us a script, with 500 words or less, along with visuals (only drawings, magazine cutouts or photographs or combination thereof). Show us how Silhouette Makes Your Love Come Alive. Be creative and have fun. No purchase necessary. All entries must be clearly marked with your name, address and telephone number. All entries will become property of Silhouette and are not returnable. **Contest closes September 28, 2001.**

Please send your entry to: **Silhouette Makes You a Star!**

In U.S.A.
P.O. Box 9069
Buffalo, NY, 14269-9069

In Canada
P.O. Box 637
Fort Erie, ON, L2A 5X3

Look for contest details on the next page, by visiting www.eHarlequin.com or request a copy by sending a self-addressed envelope to the applicable address above. Contest open to Canadian and U.S. residents who are 18 or over. Void where prohibited.

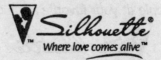

Our lucky winner's photo will appear in a Silhouette ad. Join the fun!

SRMYAS1

HARLEQUIN "SILHOUETTE MAKES YOU A STAR!" CONTEST 1308
OFFICIAL RULES
NO PURCHASE NECESSARY TO ENTER

1. To enter, follow directions published in the offer to which you are responding. Contest begins June 1, 2001, and ends on September 28, 2001. Entries must be postmarked by September 28, 2001, and received by October 5, 2001. Enter by hand-printing (or typing) on an 8 ½" x 11" piece of paper your name, address (including zip code), contest number/name and attaching a script containing 500 words or less, along with drawings, photographs or magazine cutouts, or combinations thereof (i.e., collage) on no larger than 9" x 12" piece of paper, describing how the Silhouette books make romance come alive for you. Mail via first-class mail to: Harlequin "Silhouette Makes You a Star!" Contest 1308, (in the U.S.) P.O. Box 9069, Buffalo, NY 14269-9069, (in Canada) P.O. Box 637, Fort Erie, Ontario, Canada L2A 5X3. Limit one entry per person, household or organization.

2. Contests will be judged by a panel of members of the Harlequin editorial, marketing and public relations staff. Fifty percent of criteria will be judged against script and fifty percent will be judged against drawing, photographs and/or magazine cutouts. Judging criteria will be based on the following:

    - Sincerity—25%
    - Originality and Creativity—50%
    - Emotionally Compelling—25%

    In the event of a tie, duplicate prizes will be awarded. Decisions of the judges are final.

3. All entries become the property of Torstar Corp. and may be used for future promotional purposes. Entries will not be returned. No responsibility is assumed for lost, late, illegible, incomplete, inaccurate, nondelivered or misdirected mail.

4. Contest open only to residents of the U.S. (except Puerto Rico) and Canada who are 18 years of age or older, and is void wherever prohibited by law; all applicable laws and regulations apply. Any litigation within the Province of Quebec respecting the conduct or organization of a publicity contest may be submitted to the Régie des alcools, des courses et des jeux for a ruling. Any litigation respecting the awarding of a prize may be submitted to the Régie des alcools, des courses et des jeux only for the purpose of helping the parties reach a settlement. Employees and immediate family members of Torstar Corp. and D. L. Blair, Inc., their affiliates, subsidiaries and all other agencies, entities and persons connected with the use, marketing or conduct of this contest are not eligible to enter. Taxes on prizes are the sole responsibility of the winner. Acceptance of any prize offered constitutes permission to use winner's name, photograph or other likeness for the purposes of advertising, trade and promotion on behalf of Torstar Corp., its affiliates and subsidiaries without further compensation to the winner, unless prohibited by law.

5. Winner will be determined no later than November 30, 2001, and will be notified by mail. Winner will be required to sign and return an Affidavit of Eligibility/Release of Liability/Publicity Release form within 15 days after winner notification. Noncompliance within that time period may result in disqualification and an alternative winner may be selected. All travelers must execute a Release of Liability prior to ticketing and must possess required travel documents (e.g., passport, photo ID) where applicable. Trip must be booked by December 31, 2001, and completed within one year of notification. No substitution of prize permitted by winner. Torstar Corp. and D. L. Blair, Inc., their parents, affiliates and subsidiaries are not responsible for errors in printing of contest, entries and/or game pieces. In the event of printing or other errors that may result in unintended prize values or duplication of prizes, all affected game pieces or entries shall be null and void. **Purchase or acceptance of a product offer does not improve your chances of winning.**

6. Prizes: (1) Grand Prize—A 2-night/3-day trip for two (2) to New York City, including round-trip coach air transportation nearest winner's home and hotel accommodations (double occupancy) at The Plaza Hotel, a glamorous afternoon makeover at a trendy New York spa, $1,000 in U.S. spending money and an opportunity to have a professional photo taken and appear in a Silhouette advertisement (approximate retail value: $7,000). (10) Ten Runner-Up Prizes of gift packages (retail value $50 ea.). Prizes consist of only those items listed as part of the prize. Limit one prize per person. Prize is valued in U.S. currency.

7. For the name of the winner (available after December 31, 2001) send a self-addressed, stamped envelope to: Harlequin "Silhouette Makes You a Star!" Contest 1197 Winners, P.O. Box 4200 Blair, NE 68009-4200 or you may access the www.eHarlequin.com Web site through February 28, 2002.

Contest sponsored by Torstar Corp., P.O Box 9042, Buffalo, NY 14269-9042.

SRMYAS2

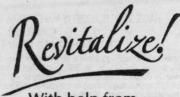